A Cry That Reached Heaven

By

Sandra Ann McFadden

Table of Contents

Introduction:

There are battles in life and challenges that seek to push our endurance, faith, and perseverance. Others are buried in their hearts silently, battling fear, doubt, and loneliness. Faith is our beacon in these moments of hardship; the darkness cannot overshadow it, and in these moments of darkness, when the world feels like it is too much to bear, faith will be the one thing to help you see through the dark and help you to remember that you are never really alone. The struggle is not the absence of faith but its victory.

But we are not alone in our struggles. We have a community of believers, a family of faith, who stand with us in our darkest hours. We believe, despite everything, that God is working behind the scenes, working all things to a greater purpose despite our weakness. We still have faith when trials overwhelm us; faith tells us that there is hope after the pain, every fallen tear is seen, and every uttered prayer is heard. We can do it through the courage to keep going despite falls and believe through faith that brighter days are ahead. This book describes how faith, supported by our community, helps us through life's most trying times.

It emphasizes difficulties in life, the power of prayer, and inner strength derived from trust in God's divine plan. In each chapter, you will read different passages from faith and strength through stories of hope, encouragement, and inspiration. Faith then reveals how hope is born from despair, courage from fear, and peace from sorrow.

Faith is an anchor in storms and uncertainty that keeps us still within the storms. It teaches that the trials we face are not meant to break us, but cutting the iron out of the fire will mold us stronger, wiser, more compassionate, more able, and more in tune with that love that gave us our lives. Often, the most incredible stories of victory, as they pertain to scripture or life, stem from seasons of suffering. Faith is the brightest in those valleys of despair.

Even when we do not know which way to go, God is already traveling ahead of us and preparing our way.

No matter how deep your struggles are, how hard you feel, or how long you have been on the ground, cry out loud to God and know that he always listens. It is in your darkest moments that you are not forgotten. What you face, a power greater than yourself loves, cherishes, and guides you. With faith, you can find the power to keep moving ahead because God's love, grace, and wisdom will lead you through the storm, all the way to the battle, and through every doubt. Faith is not just a belief; it's a transformative force that can turn despair into hope, fear into courage, and sorrow into peace.

Chapter 1: The Reality of Life's Struggles

Life is a journey filled with its own set of struggles, a universal experience that often catches us off guard. These struggles can take many forms: financial, emotional, physical, and spiritual. They can consume us, leaving us feeling unworthy, stupid, and useless. The burdens that come with these difficulties can make life seem impossible. We are shaken to our core by the storms we face, wondering if we are strong enough to weather them.

Some of these struggles drive people into despondency, isolation, and hopelessness. Perhaps, we feel that we are no longer loved, that we are forgotten, that it is all uncomfortable, and that we are in the dark. However, a profound truth rises from the darkest times: suffering and struggles are not meaningless. Our true character is formed in them. They are tools of growth that teach us more about ourselves, our faith, and our purpose. These challenges help us understand what it means to trust and surrender to God's will.

The Power of Suffering: A Path to Self-Discovery

There is an adage that hardship makes us. However, how does suffering lead to a person's growth? The reality is that pain is a challenging and uncomfortable teacher. We find out who we are only through suffering. When you have lost everything and have nothing to depend on, you are pushed to look within. In these moments of vulnerability, we start to know our deepest wishes, values, and resilience potential.

It is an often-tricky self-discovery process that does not occur quickly. Usually, we resist it. We refuse to make sense of why; we do not allow ourselves to understand what we are going through; we do everything we can to fight against the pain, shed its intensity, wish it away, and hope for an easy escape. However, actual growth proclaims that we have to confront our struggles. We become more assertive on the other side of the process by facing our fears and insecurities.

Faith in the Face of Adversity: Biblical Stories of Strength

The Bible contains many of the greatest stories about people exercising faith in the face of suffering. Not many people talk about what leads to the lonely places, the dark forests, caves, and aloneness in general, which can be filled with. Job, for example, was a man who lost his entire wealth, family, and health. Despite such terrible losses, Job did not curse God or lose faith. His story reveals that to have faith is not to be free from suffering, but to trust in God regardless of our circumstances.

Job's story is not an anomaly. The Bible consists of stories of individuals who endured horrible struggles but came out wiser, stronger, and more faithful to God. For instance, Joseph was betrayed by his brothers, he was sold into slavery, and falsely imprisoned. Despite these injustices, however, he kept faith and trust in God. However, Joseph's suffering did not all happen in vain. This was elevated by God and used to place him in a powerful position, where he saved many lives during the famine.

These stories demonstrate one thing without a doubt: struggles and suffering do not mark the end of our story. They are the chapters that prepare us for the blessings yet to come. Refining us, they make us into people meant to become.

The Question of Why: Understanding the Purpose of Struggles

When going through tough times, dwelling on feeling like some divine power is punishing us is natural. Why does God let trials get into our lives? It is an unfortunate truth of life, a constant question in the human psyche: Why do bad things happen to good people? Often, these questions cause a crisis of faith, a feeling that God has left us or has stopped listening to us. Maybe we begin to doubt the meaning of our lives and our dreams. Although they are difficult questions, they may also grant a deeper spiritual understanding.

Human beings, as such, view their struggles narrowly. We only see the pain and loss, that which has been taken from us. God's view is eternal and also broad. Romans 8:28 reminds us that "all things work together for the good of those who love Him." This does not guarantee that every trial is easy or pleasant, but we know that God works beyond our sight and view, taking even our suffering and using it for his greater purpose.

During times of need, note that God is not far or unconcerned. He is there to work for our good. Knowing this still does not alleviate the pain, but it provides hope. It has given us the confidence that something bigger is happening when we cannot see it. Though we may not always know why we are being made to go through a trial, we can be sure it is happening for a reason, the bigger picture of which will result in our growth, healing, and restoration.

Finding Strength in God: Trusting His Plan

The simplest of questions, why do we suffer, has no perfect answer. One thing is sure: God's plan is perfect even when it may not seem so to us. When we suffer, we must believe in His plan and rely on our faith. God does not say life will not hurt; he promises never to leave us. 'According to Psalm 34:18, 'The Lord is near to the brokenhearted and saves the crushed in spirit.

It is easy to believe God has deserted us when we feel overwhelmed. The truth is, however, that He is closest to us when we are at our lowest. Therefore, He walks us through our valley of pain and comforts and strengthens us when we need it most. Although we cannot always feel His presence, He is there, steering us to healing and newness of life.

When we are suffering, we are invited to get closer to God, find comfort in Him, and have confidence that all the strength we need to continue is available. Having this kind of trust is not always easy, especially when the road ahead seems uncertain. However, faith in God is the only way to be at peace and have hope even in the most challenging times.

The Gift of Faith: Growing Through Trials

Faith is not a passive belief but an active belief. When we experience trials, we can trust Him or turn away and despair. This is not always an easy choice; our trust in God strengthens us to overcome our struggles.

According to James 1:2-4, "the testing of your faith produces perseverance." Do not give up; perseverance must complete its work so that you may be mature and complete, not lacking anything." The hardship is not about avoiding it; it is often about growing through it. Your trials are not to break you but to refine you. They cause us to stumble, but they also develop our perseverance, character, and the love of God deep within us.

As we go through life, we must remember that we have been given faith. You can only see beyond your circumstances through faith and believe the best God has in store for your life. Whichever way we are struggling, it is not in vain. They are an opportunity for us to grow in faith, grow closer to the God we have, and be the people He means for us to be.

The Role of Community in Times of Struggle

We have a gift as believers; one of our community's greatest gifts is support. We are quickly propelled to isolation and seclusion, especially when facing trials, thinking we must go through the struggle alone. However, the Bible tells us we are not meant to carry things ourselves. The Bible says in Galatians 6:2, 'Carry one another's burdens; in this way you will fulfill the law of Christ.'

Hard times are times for us to turn to other brothers and sisters in Christ to carry us. If I know someone in need, their prayers, efforts to bring them reminders that they are not alone, encouragement, and practical help are a blessing. The existence and presence of these people are just as valid as that of God walking with us through our struggles. He uses the people around us to give us comfort and strength. Community reminds us that we are part of something larger than ourselves, and we can have hope that we are among people walking through the same waters.

Embracing Struggles with Faith

Life's struggles are a given, but they do not make you. It is the way that we respond to those struggles that makes us a man of character or not. Suffering helps us understand who we are and who God himself is. So when we cannot see a way forward, we learn to trust that He has a plan.

God is with us whenever life's tests come our way. He is close to the brokenhearted and goes beside us in the storm. This is not in vain. It is the stepping stone for a deeper, stronger, and closer walk with God.

Therefore, faith is not the absence of suffering but the trust to suffer through it. If we can learn to surrender ourselves to God's will, we will become more like Him, more potent, wiser, more beautiful inside, and more capable of facing life as it happens. Finally, we will only feel the fullness of God's grace and love through the struggle and experience the peace that surpasses all understanding.

Embracing Pain as a Tool for Transformation

The most incredible truth I have learned as life has hit me is that pain is not an obstacle to avoid but a tool for transformation. By enduring pain, we are refined (as one refines precious metals in the fire and on the anvil). Just like we purify gold by fire, our hearts are purified through the fire of trials and tribulations that come upon us.

This is not always visible while the change is happening. In the transformation process, we seldom see the changes occurring within us. With time, we start realizing how much pain we have molded ourselves into. There is growth in our empathy, compassion, and understanding. Because of the simple things, we have a deeper appreciation for the simple joys of life and attain a more remarkable ability to bounce back from the challenges ahead.

When looked at through the eyes of faith, pain is not a senseless experience. We were not given a miracle for no reason; it serves a higher purpose, brings us closer to God, and assists us in becoming the people we are supposed to be. This view allows us to handle all those trials we struggle with, not as a void but as a plan, from God's plan that it is ultimately for the sake of our growth and a sheer transformation of our lives.

The Role of Prayer and Meditation in Overcoming Struggles

Prayer and meditation become priceless weapons when helping us keep our faith and strength in times of struggle. Praying is our line straight to God. We can say our pain in prayer, ask for comfort, and seek guidance. Prayer in times of despair is simply surrendering what words might remain. In quiet times, we commune with God and find solace and peace because we are not alone.

Mediation also helps us navigate the difficulties of life. Through meditation on the Word of God, we can gain strength and encouragement from Scripture. Meditation helps us clear our minds and think about God's words and promises, showing us that He is faithful and full of love. Meditation is beneficial when one is uncertain and needs clarity and direction toward a healing and hopeful place to walk again.

Prayer and meditation together build the spiritual foundation we need when going through hell. They remind us of the peace of God, which transcends human understanding and is always available to us. Prayer and meditation help us channel a source of strength much more significant than our abilities.

The Importance of Forgiveness During Times of Struggle

Another essential part of overcoming the obstacles that life presents is the act of forgiveness. Resentment and anger toward others are easy when we are hurt by others or betrayed. While natural, these emotions can keep us weighed down and standing still in our healing journey. Forgiveness, however, offers a path to freedom.

Indeed, in Matthew 6:14-15, Jesus tells us, 'For if you forgive other people when they sin against you, your heavenly Father will also forgive you. If you do not forgive others, your Father will not forgive your sins." Forgiveness is not something you do to condone the wrongs you have done to yourself, but to free the bitterness and anger that they have in your heart. It is letting go of the past and allowing yourself to have and receive the peace and healing God is offering.

The process of forgiveness is usually complex and ongoing. It is not overnight, and we might have to keep revisiting our pain. These things happen in this world, but through the power of the Holy Spirit, we can have the strength to forgive when it appears to be impossible. As we forgive, we relieve ourselves from bearing unforgiveness and let God work in our hearts to restore whatever needs to be repaired.

The Power of Hope: Looking Beyond the Present Struggle

Behind every dark hour, we are sustained with hope, a powerful force. Hope is the belief that good days will return even if the current days are hard. Hope allows us to bear hardship graciously, with purpose and determination, because we know we have a plan from God and that our suffering is not the final chapter of our lives.

The promise of Romans 15:13 should give us all: "May the God of hope fill you with all joy and peace as you trust in Him, so that you may overflow with hope by the power of the Holy Spirit." We do not create hope ourselves, but God gives it to us. As we cannot see, we hope His plan for our lives is good. He will take away the ashes of our pain and bring beauty.

Hope is everything; it gives us the strength to move on despite being on a road with no end in sight. It brings us back to the fact that God is alongside us in everything and shall never leave or forsake us. Hope serves us as this divine substance so that when we hold onto hope, we can confidently endure the trials of life, because in the end, God will bring our healing, restoration, and ultimately victory.

Finding Meaning in the Struggle: The Purpose Behind Pain

So naturally, we have to question: 'Why suffer?' or 'Why be afflicted with pain?' We might ask ourselves, what is the point of struggling when it seems to serve no purpose and overwhelms us? However, Scripture reminds us that God works good out of our pain. As per the 2 Corinthians 1:3-4, the Bible says, "Praise be to the God and Father of our Lord Jesus Christ, the Father of compassion and the God of all comfort, who comforts us in all our troubles, so that we can comfort those in any trouble with the comfort we have received from God."

We struggle not just for ourselves but also to strengthen others who are going through the same things. We can provide others the same comfort when we know God's comfort amid our pain. In a way, our pain becomes empathy, leading us to relate to suffering people and give them the hope and encouragement they need.

Also, our battles make us better; they teach us patience, humility, and reliance upon the Lord. They remove our self-reliance; we must rely on God for our strength. Through those lessons, we learn how to become more like Christ, who suffered much for our sake. As a result, with struggle, we are molded into vessels of His love and grace and are thus better able to serve others.

The Eternal Perspective: Keeping Our Eyes on the Bigger Picture

When we suffer, we are most prone to miss the big picture. Our pain is all-consuming, and we cannot see outside of our circumstances at that moment. However, as believers, we are supposed to take our struggles from an eternal perspective. We understand that this life is temporary and that the pain we will endure here is nothing compared to the glory yet to come.

Paul says in 2 Corinthians 4:17-18, 'For our light affliction, which is but for a moment, in His sight is producing for us an everlasting weight of glory that is beyond all comparison.' We are looking not at what can be seen but what cannot. For what can be seen is temporary, but what cannot be seen is eternal." It reminds you that it is infinite and that your suffering has a purpose, not only now. It shapes us for eternity, and we are prepared for the joy, peace, and fulfillment ahead of us in the presence of God.

However, more often than not, through the struggle, we are encouraged to keep our eyes on the hope of eternal life. This way of looking at things helps us patiently suffer the trials of this world, for we are not being killed in vain. However, we also have the strength to see through the longest roads to the painful ones because we know the reward will far outweigh the pain.

Moving Forward with Faith and Strength

Life is filled with struggles, but God's faithfulness is absolute, too. While we are alive with the pain, He is here with us, comforting us and giving us strength and hope. Struggles in our lives help us trust Him more, depend on His grace, and learn the essence of faith.

In our days, we remember that we did not walk alone. The struggles we face in life are not insignificant; God is with us every step of the way. Our struggles are used to refine us, bring us closer to Him, and prepare us to receive what He will put into our lives. There is a reason for our pain. That is part of God's larger plan of what He is making us to be.

However, we overcome life's struggles through faith, prayer, meditation, forgiveness, and hope. Lastly, we become stronger, wiser, and more faithful, thus prepared for whatever lies before us. Our struggles do not mark the end of our story; they are the beginning of our new face and continuing story. As we learn about God's love to the full, the strength of our faith, and the hope of a brighter tomorrow.

Chapter 2: The Silent Tears – When No One Sees

There are a large number of struggles that remain silent. As everyone else does, we cry with our backs against the closed door. We cry alone while passing the closed door, thinking no one sees, cares, or understands how painful we feel. People do not notice how unbearable loneliness is when suffering and how onerous our burdens are. Though we still feel lost, we brave it against others, but feel lost, consumed, and in pain. The silent tears, though, are not foreign to Father God. He is witness to every pain we go through; every prayer that choked in our throats, and every unuttered cry when the world is asleep over us.

Hesitation is always a moment in which a change is longed for, a moment of faith's inception. This is a moment when the world is still; when God wants to hear our hearts speak in stillness, and He is there in the stillness of the heart. As God quietly kisses your tears upon your cheek, you can hear Him whisper, present. In our sorrow, God whispers the sweetest promise of companionship.

He ignores our grief and sorrow. Instead, He comes up close to us in our days of lowest. Scripture assures the truth: God stores every tear in a bottle (Psalm 56:8) and neither can nor will He not care for us. He is not cold or far from our sorrow; He is a Father who takes it in His heart.

God sees our pain even when He understands it cannot be understood. He knows how deep all of our struggles are below the surface. He knows our disappointments, fears, and brokenness. But it's easy to think the world does not care, does not want to talk to us, does not care to listen to our stories, is too busy, doesn't care about our struggles and heartaches; yet, there is a profound truth that we can hold on to: God cares, He sees and is with us.

A Silent Struggle, Yet a Mighty Strength

Many silent tears are caused by a personal battle others may not know about or notice. In other words, we don't talk about it, but the weight of our emotions usually seems unbearable. We doubt whether anyone is interested in us, but God keeps awake and watches over us, His eyes on our needs as the world sleeps. Finally, the Word of God offers a comforting truth: "He knows the way that I take; when He has tested me, I will come forth as gold" (Job 23:10).

This verse sets the tone that your struggles are not in vain. God allows us to walk through the fire instead of consuming and purifying us. Suffering's fire weeds out impurities and gives us strength we never knew we had. Our silent tears dry us. We don't understand it at the time, but they are making us into the people God has fashioned us to be.

The Story of Hannah – A Woman's Silent Desperation

Although they were silent in their suffering, God did not forget them. So, the story of Hannah in 1 Samuel 1 is one of the most potent examples of quiet pain. Hannah's story will speak to anyone who has ever felt forgotten, left out, or desperately needed something they cannot have.

Hannah was struggling, not a surface struggle, but a soul-wrenching battle. This sorrow was compounded for her, as she was a woman unable to conceive, and as society had expectations of her. In those days, a woman was sometimes judged on her ability to bear children, and Hannah's inability to conceive left her feeling incomplete. Although she had a good husband, her heart was set on a child. Her deep sorrow forced her to pour out her anguish in the temple and in the privacy of her soul to call to God.

She did not cry out in her desperation, internalising her pain and moving her lips in silent prayer. Eli, the priest, watched her and mistook her for a drunk. But God saw her pain. Her soft, silent prayer was heard from the depths of her heart and by the Almighty. God answered her prayer in His perfect timing, and after some time, she conceived and bore a son named Samuel.

As if her story were insufficient, heaven never takes even the impression of silently suffering lightly. Likewise, God seeth Hannah, He seeth thee. Just as they heard you, He listened to her unspoken cries. He also promised that as He answered her, He would reply to you in His perfect time.

The Struggle That Births Life

Struggle is needed for life to exist. Imagine this: Right at the moment of conception, the male seed and female egg must undergo a challenge; there has to be a breakthrough for life to be born in the mother's womb. To struggle is to live, and through the beauty of creation, life is allowed and begins out of the struggle of life. With a battle, God's most incredible creation Is born from darkness into life.

What about the miracle of conception: the male seed that, after all, battles for survival against all odds and just fights, breaks all barriers to get to the female egg to bring life into existence. First, like everything, life is born in the darkest place of this world, the womb, where the baby is growing and developing for nine months. In other words, the womb, which appeared to be a limited space, is the space of creation, growth, and preparation. It's dark, it's also a nurturing dark. The baby is born after nine months, not without difficulty, but with the struggle of travailing pain. In a child's cry, ascending to heaven, is that birth moment, so painful yet beautiful.

This cry is more than that of a newborn; the victory cry comes out of the defeat of the dark and is the first sound ever heard. So too is the life process that includes our struggles. We enter this world, a world of challenge, and we cry silently for the pain we are experiencing. Yet, like the labor of childbirth, our struggles become more significant, offering a nobler cause for living and for dying. Such times exist because God prepares us for something even greater.

The Struggle of Life from Birth to the Grave

Birth through the grave is a real struggle. There is a challenge in each moment of life. Its struggles in childhood, adolescence, adulthood, and old age are yet to be neglected. There is a new set of obstacles, new opportunities to grow, new strength, and new faith in each phase of life. Psalm 34:1 reads: King David, a man who was very familiar with much struggle in his life, says, 'I will bless the Lord at all times; His praise shall continually be in my mouth." In his understanding of the hardships of life, David understood that God's presence was present at all times, and was worthy of praise, regardless of the season.

In Psalm 139:14, we have the truth about the struggle of life: 'I praise you because I am fearfully and wonderfully made.' The goal of this verse is to tell us that we are created with a purpose and value despite our trials. Struggling does not make us weak but strong and powerful. We have been fearfully and wonderfully made; every trial is perfect for a purpose, and even the refining, shaping, and preparation are being done by God for His greater purpose.

Faith amid Suffering

One thing we can hope to learn from learning to have faith amid suffering is understanding silent struggles. Why does God allow us to go through such trials? For centuries, believers and nonbelievers alike have been perplexed by suffering. But suffering is not a sign of God's absence; far from it, suffering is a sign of God's molding hand, as discerned through the lens of Scripture.

Jesus Himself faced great suffering. He was "a man of sorrows and acquainted with grief" (Isaiah 53:3). Christ knows more than anyone else the weight of sorrow and pain. There was a purpose in his suffering. We have the ultimate redemption because He lived the ultimate pain on the cross. Going through His suffering teaches us to find strength through our trials. God isn't promising us an easy life, but promises to walk us through life. Jesus says in Matthew 11:28, "All you that are weary and are heavy burdened, come to me and I will give you rest."

As Christ's suffering ended in resurrection and hope, our suffering also ends in new growth and understanding. Even the silent tears that flow in the darkest moments have meaning; they may as well deliver new life, just like the pain of childbirth.

The Power of Prayer in Silence

When the world feels like it's weighing infinitely on your shoulders, but you cannot speak the words, it is essential to understand that prayer has power. Not all prayer involves saying loud words with perfect language; the most powerful prayer is whispered in the quiet of the heart. God hears our hearts. He hears the words not said, the cries never uttered, the pleas never spoken, and never found their way past the bottom of our soul.

'In the same way, the Spirit helps us in our weakness' (the verse through the Bible app Fighting Fear of the Future is Romans 8:26). And he who searches our hearts knows the mind of the Spirit, because the Spirit intercedes for God's people by the will of God." Our silent tears, those unspeakable cries that bring about tears, God's own Holy Spirit intercedes. It is incredible to know that God is on our side, working on our behalf, answering our unspoken cries even in our weakest times.

Finding Peace Amidst the Struggle

At the deepest levels of faith in silent suffering, one of the most profound things is finding peace. It seems counterintuitive, but your peace is not reliant on your circumstances when you trust God through the struggles of life. As Philippians 4:7 states, "the peace of God which passes all understanding shall guard your hearts and minds through Christ Jesus." The peace is not in the external things, but in an internal trust that God is in control.

Whether through tears, struggles, or even heartache, God's peace is available for us. It keeps despair and hopelessness away from our hearts. We have the strength to suffer, the courage to persevere, for God is with us in this peace, even in our most silent moments of sorrow.

Embracing the Journey – Your Silent Tears Matter

We must understand that these silent tears will never go wasted. They matter. They are a part of the journey God has chosen to use to refine and shape us into the people He's called us to be. He sees when nobody else does—God. God listens when all else seems to hear. And God is closest to us when we are the most alone.

Remember, there is never a struggle in this life that you have to go through alone. God is always working on your behalf. He hears you, and He sees you. Your silent tears have meaning. They are not in vain. At the end of those days, we will have a clearer understanding of God's love, faithfulness, and perfect plan for your life.

The Power of Vulnerability in the Journey

In our culture, vulnerability is considered a weakness. We are
taught to be strong, to hide our tears, and to be strong and
carry on, showing no pain. Vulnerability is a weakness, but in
the kingdom of God. To God, a burden is not meant to be
carried alone. We were made to rely on Him, drag our
difficulties to Him, and find comfort in His presence.

When Lazarus died, Jesus showed vulnerability when He wept at
the tomb (John 11:35). Despite raising Lazarus from the dead,
He still wept. He didn't hide His emotions and did not conceal
His feelings. No matter how painful, he allowed himself to feel
the pain and sorrow of the moment. Doing so, He also showed
us it is OK to mourn, to cry, and to feel deeply. When we are
vulnerable, it is a doorway for God to come and give us healing.

When we are vulnerably made open to God, God enters our
deepest places. Our tears, raw emotions, and brokenness will
not cause him to take off. He is closest to us in those moments
of vulnerability. In our sorrow, he consoles us and gives us the
power to bear.

The Role of Faith in Silent Suffering

Faith is not about being confident that God will take us out of
our pain, but about trusting that God is in our pain. There are
moments of silent suffering; these test our faith. It's easy to
believe in times of good, but it is at the heart of sorrow that our
faith is refined.

According to Hebrews 11:1, faith is confidence in what we hope
for and assurance about what we do not see. Believing in God
to change your circumstances is a part of faith, but faith also
depends on His presence when things look hopeless. Our silent
tears are our silent worship of a God that we believe has His

character, love, and promise that He will never leave or forsake us.

It may not make sense why we suffer, but we can comfort ourselves that God is sovereign and is working all things together for our good (Romans 8:28). Faith is knowing that even in silent pain, God is working. We are prepared, sharpened, and honed for what is next.

The Transformative Power of Pain

There is never any reasonable time to be in pain, but it has the power to change us. Praise be to the God and Father of our Lord Jesus Christ, the Father of compassion and the God of all comfort, who comforts us in all our troubles, so that we can comfort those in any problem with the comfort we receive from God (2 Corinthians 1:3-4).

Pain is a tool given to us to transform ourselves when surrendered to God. What we learn from our struggles is compassion, empathy, and understanding. That is important because whenever we go through pain, we can help people dealing with similar difficulties more effectively. Though isolating, our tears have always been a bridge to others. We can bind with and comfort the one in pain by suffering ourselves.

For sure, this transformation process is not immediate, and it does not feel easy. However, over time, God transforms the tragedy of our suffering into shaping us into the character of Christ (compassion, patience, love). As gold needs the fire to be purged, we must likewise undergo the fires of life to be refined. This is the process, as we are vessels of God's grace, healing instruments for the broken world.

A New Perspective on Struggles

The more we perceive our struggles, the worse the experience becomes. Suffering consumes us when we look at it as pointless or without hope. However, when we rethink and take a perspective of faith in our challenges, we come to realise that our pain serves a purpose.

God never wastes our suffering. He takes every tear, trial, and hurtful moment to create more of His purpose in our lives. Perhaps we do not always know how or why, but we can trust that He is working. According to 2 Corinthians 4:17, Paul says, 'For our momentary light affliction is producing for us an absolutely surpassing and exceedingly bitter but glorious gain.'

They are our temporary struggles, but eternally impactful on our lives and others. Struggles are sometimes a part of the story of God's redemption, but they become so when we endure our part with faith. Our silent tears are not wasted; we will reap a harvest of the kingdom for His glory.

The Healing Power of Hope

Hope is our anchor when we suffer silently. Hope is not removing pain; it is the knowledge that greater things are coming amid the worst pain. That bot hopes that God works in our lives, but we cannot see it, which gives us the might to continue.

For we know (Greek: oida) the process: First suffering; then, through suffering, perseverance; and then, by perseverance, character; and from character, hope — Romans 5:3-4 (ESV). Hope is born while suffering. This is what God is working in my life, making me into who he has destined me to become.

Even so, in our silent tears, we can hope that God has not given up on us. We cannot see the whole picture, but he is always working. One day, we will look back at the struggles and realise how they were intended for our good and His glory.

From Silent Tears to Joyful Triumph

The silent tears we shed are painful and do not make us who we are. They are part of the story, but they will not be the end of it. God promises to change our mourning to joy. However, Psalm 30:5 promises, Weeping may endure for a night, but rejoicing comes in the morning.

Today, the tears will be with us; they will not remain forever. As the morning always follows the darkest of nights, so will joy follow our sorrow. God will wipe away every tear from our eyes (Revelation 21:4). The struggles and the victory awaited are eternal.

We are being prepared for the joy to come through our silent tears. It is testing our faith and refining and strengthening it. However, He will do what is perfect for us in His time, and we will experience victory in God's love and faithfulness.

Faced with unanswered and unanswerable suffering, Doing Church and Cancelled Church by Pete Scazzero offers a refreshing assessment. Part One of this book focuses on Walking in His Presence ('finding strength in the journey'). Part Two has the thematic focus of 'Savoring Scripture and Conversation,' each culminating in a Part published chapter and a Part evaluated blank chapter.

As we continue through life and its struggles, we will never forget that we are never truly alone. During our silent moments in pain, God is with us in our sorrow. He sees tears, he hears cries, and he knows unspoken words.

May we know that our trip is meant to be. God's divine plan includes every tear, struggle, and moment of pain. He is making it all to define, polish, and set us up for something better. Moreover, on this road through life, He is with us—every footstep taken, we do it in His company.

The Hidden Battles – When the World Does not See

Every day, we face an unofficial war, an inconspicuous fight that takes place inside that no one may notice. Without realising it, we walk through life wearing smiles, saying 'I am fine' when asked how we are doing, yet in them lies doubt, fear, and sadness that we battle from within. Some of the most brutal battles to fight are the silent ones because there is no visible scar or outward sign that one is fighting a storm within.

But God sees. He pierces through the veneer that we wear for the world to see. He knows, too, those burdens we carry and the weight we bear within our hearts. As Psalm 34:18 says, 'The Lord is close to the brokenhearted and saves the crushed in spirit.' He never sees us unseen, even when others do not see us. He stands beside us in the hidden struggles where we believe we have nothing to give, providing strength and comfort.

Today, if you find an unseen battle to carry, you do not have to carry alone. God is with you. He is your defender, refuge, and present help in times of trouble (Psalm 46:1). Bring your burdens to Him. Even if you are quiet to the world, your cries are heard in the heavens.

The Night Season – When the Soul Feels Weary

As nature's patterns of day and night cycles result in light and darkness, so does the soul experience periods of light and darkness. At times, our faith seems strong, our hearts are full of hope, and joy is close at hand. However, there are times when darkness appears to be painted before us indefinitely, when prayers are seemingly unanswered, and when our souls are tired from the hardships of life.

The night season is hard because you do not usually see the end. However, the Bible reassures that nothing is too dark for God to come over. He says in Isaiah 45:3, "I will give you the treasures of darkness and secret riches, so you may know that I am the Lord, who calls you by your name, the God of Israel (KJV)."

That means something valuable is produced in even the most painful seasons. Our silent tears are not idle but water the soil of our faith while preparing for a day of future joy and strength. As we know, there is one journey in life that leads from evening to morning, and as one day's struggles lead to another, we live in a new season of healing and restoration.

The Purpose in Pain – When Suffering Has Meaning

One thing that life teaches us with pain is one of the greatest. Although we desire to do without it, pain shapes us in ways that comfort can never match. It deepens our emotionality, improves our character, and improves our reliance on God in several ways that we could never have made.

Joseph is an example found in the book of Genesis. His life had been hard: he had been sold into slavery, betrayed by his brothers, and wrongly imprisoned. However, God had a purpose in all of it. Joseph's suffering was not in vain, and it put him in the correct position to become a leader in Egypt and save many lives during the famine. In Genesis 50:20, he told them when he finally came face to face with his brothers, "What you meant for evil, God meant for good, to bring it about that many people should be kept alive."

The same is true for us. Everything we go through today is not to no avail. He is using them to refine us for something greater.

However, we cannot fathom what He is working for right now, and yet we must have faith that He is working something beautiful out of this pain.

The Comfort of His Presence – You Are Not Alone

The enemy will tell one of the biggest lies during our moments of suffering... that we are alone. No one cares about or understands us; even God has forgotten us, he tells us. Far from it, however.

As is stated in Deuteronomy 31:8, "The Lord himself goes before you and will be with you; he will never leave you nor forsake you." Do not be afraid; do not be discouraged."

God is not far from us in our suffering. He is near. In life's trials, he walks beside us, holds us when we are weak, and whispers words of encouragement when we are tempted to give in. His presence keeps us steady in the storm.

Moreover, be comforted that He is there even in the silence. He works behind the scenes, orchestrating a plan for your good even when you cannot feel Him. Lean into His presence. Let Him take the burdens that are too heavy to bear.

The Strength to Keep Going – Choosing Faith Over Fear

We are exhausted from life's struggles; we no longer know if we can move forward as we used to. However, God calls us to walk by faith and not sight (2 Corinthians 5:7), which means that even when the situation looks bleak, we choose to trust Him. We take a step forward in faith even when in fear; it paralyses us.

This is beautifully illustrated by Peter, who then walked on water (Matthew 14:22-33). Peter kept his eyes on Jesus, and if he looked only at Jesus, he could have done the impossible; he walked on water. However, he started to sink the instant fear took him.

Ultimately, we are not overcome because our eyes are fixed on Jesus, and raging waves cannot pull us under. When we are weak, He is our strength; when the way ahead is unclear, He is our guide. Even when it feels like giving up is the only solution, we can continue with Him.

The Promise of Restoration – A New Beginning Awaits

Today's pain is not the end of our story. God is a God of restoration. He fixes what is broken and turns it into wholeness. He takes mourning, creates joy and ashes, and creates beauty, despair, and hope.

It is an incredible promise, but the level of detail comes from Joel 2:25: "I will restore to you the years that the swarming locust has eaten." God can restore whatever we have lost: peace, joy, relationships, and dreams. He can take the most painful parts of our lives and make something beautiful out of them.

It is not an overnight restoration, but the restoration is coming. The ones we have cried without making a sound will not be forgotten, the ones we have whispered are not ignored, and the ones we have withstood will not be wasted. A new beginning awaits. Regarding His promises, He is faithful in finishing the work in us He has already begun (Philippians 1:6).

Rising from the Ashes – Walking into Victory

The things we go through shape us, but do not define us. They define us by what we do in response. Or do we break ourselves on them, with the wherewithal to stand for something always better?

God promises: "beauty for ashes, the oil of joy for mourning, the garment of praise for the spirit of heaviness" (Isaiah 61:3). What was supposed to be for harm he turns into good. He gives us the strength to return from our pain to our victory.

Regardless of what you have gone through, you are stronger than you know. You are loved beyond measure. Your tears have not been silent in vain. God is with you as you are guided and prepared for something bigger than you can imagine.

Chapter 3: Seeking God in Desperation

The Crossroads of Crisis and Faith

None of us wants to go into desperation, but desperation is holy ground where we have some of our most profound encounters with God. We are sent to the Almighty's arms when every human struggle ends—when the counsel of friends, the comfort of family, and even the best medical advice can accomplish no more. We sent them there, hardly daring and fearful, but seeking. At the intersection of hopelessness and faith, something sacred unfolds. Only in the darkest hours do we feel light break in the most unexpected ways.

Many believers will say that their most powerful moments with God were not in the time of plenty, but in the pit of despair. Why? Desperation is a nasty mistress and has a way of cutting out distractions and relying on oneself. It extinguishes the fog and makes divine space for it. It propels us to pray with larger props, cry more pressingly, and hunt more animatedly than ever. This is not simply an emotional chaos: it is a spiritual alignment. God picks up His most momentum in those raw, honest, and broken moments.

The Woman with the Issue of Blood: A Portrait of Relentless Faith

Let us revisit the profound story found in Mark 5:25-34. An unnamed but unforgettable woman symbolizes undeterred faith in the face of relentless suffering. She had been bleeding for twelve long years. In ancient Jewish culture, her condition made her ritually unclean (Leviticus 15:25-27), which meant she was likely cut off from family, religious gatherings, and all forms of societal interaction. She was isolated—physically, emotionally, and spiritually.

Not only was she sick, but she was also financially depleted. The Scripture says she had "suffered many things of many physicians," and instead of getting better, she only grew worse. She had exhausted all her resources and had nothing left but faith.

Moreover, what did she do with that bit of remaining faith? She turned it into action.

She had heard of Jesus, and that alone sparked hope. She must have reasoned, "If I can just touch His clothes, I will be healed." This was not superstition—a belief that broke protocol and defied logic. She did not ask to be noticed, and she did not need to have a conversation. All she wanted was one touch, one act of faith.

She pushed through the crowd, risking shame or punishment, reaching for His garment. Moreover, in that very instant, the bleeding stopped. She knew it. Jesus knew it. Power had gone out from Him.

He stopped. "Who touched me?" The disciples were baffled—many were pressing in, yet Jesus distinguished one touch: the touch of desperation mixed with faith.

Trembling, the woman stepped forward and told Him everything. Instead of rebuking her, Jesus called her "Daughter"—a term of love, acceptance, and identity. "Your faith has healed you. Go in peace and be freed from your suffering."

This was more than physical healing. It was total restoration—emotional, spiritual, and societal. Her story reminds us that when we reach out to God in our lowest moments, He does not just stop what He is doing—He transforms our situation entirely.

Desperation as a Divine Invitation

It is tempting to view desperation as weakness. Society often teaches us to be strong, independent, and self-reliant. However, desperation is not disqualification in the Kingdom of God—it is an invitation. It is the knock on heaven's door that refuses to go unanswered.

The Psalms are filled with cries from David, a man after God's heart, who was often in desperate straits. Whether fleeing Saul, mourning a lost child, or lamenting his sins, David's cries reached the ears of God. In Psalm 34:17-18, he writes, "The righteous cry out, and the Lord hears them; He delivers them from all their troubles. The Lord is close to the brokenhearted and saves those crushed in spirit."

Notice the pattern: crying out, being heard, and receiving deliverance. That is the holy cycle of desperation.

Fasting and Prayer: Catalysts for Divine Encounter

Fasting and prayer are set as they are famous for desperation, sometimes compelling us to do this. They are not religious duties; they are also spiritual weapons. Together, we can unlock spiritual breakthroughs that we cannot imagine.

Esther knew this. She did not rush to the king's court upon her people's being on the brink of termination. Instead, all the Jews in Susa fasted with her for three days. So she knew the risk in coming before the king unbidden—it could be death. However, she also knew that approaching her King in heaven would have been favorable. Then, her desperation went to boldness, and her boldness translated to national salvation.

So even when it was a matter of life and death, Daniel prayed thrice daily. He had not renounced his faith in this lion's den, but it was because he had not given it up. He was fearless because of his desperation to have God's presence more than the king's decree.

The body fasts, but the spirit is filled. It says, "God, You are more important than the food, the comfort, and the convenience. Only I need you more than anything; that is what I need you to know." If this cry is a true yearning, heaven listens to it.

Modern Stories of Seeking in Desperation

Even today, stories abound of people who found God when all else failed. A woman battling cancer with no treatment options left prays fervently and finds peace—and, remarkably, a miracle of healing. A man losing his job, home, and marriage falls to his knees and encounters Christ in the silence. A prisoner in solitary confinement receives a Bible and has a life-changing encounter with Jesus.

These are not fairy tales. These are testimonies—modern-day reflections of biblical truths. God has not changed. The same Jesus who healed the woman with the issue of blood is healing hearts and lives today.

The Power of Persistent Pursuit

Jesus often taught about persistence. In Luke 18, he tells the story of a persistent widow who kept returning to a judge for justice. Though the judge did not fear God or respect people, he granted her request because of her relentlessness. Jesus used this parable to illustrate that God, who is loving, will surely respond to His children who cry out to Him day and night.

There is power in not giving up. Desperation may bring us to our knees, but persistent faith keeps us there until the answer comes. It is the kind of pursuit that wrestles with God like Jacob and says, "I will not let you go unless you bless me!" (Genesis

32:26). It is the cry of Hannah at the temple, weeping bitterly and praying for a child. Her desperation gave birth to Samuel, one of Israel's greatest prophets.

What Desperation Reveals About Us—and About God

When we are desperate, we find out who we are—and who God is.

We learn how limited our control is, discover the depth of our need, and realize that God is not a last resort; He is the only trustworthy source of help.

Desperation does not scare God. It draws Him near. Psalm 145:18 says, "The Lord is near to all who call on Him, to all who call on Him in truth." This kind of calling is born out of desperation, when the pretense disappears and only truth remains.

God's Response to Desperate Seekers

When people in Scripture sought God desperately, He responded:

Hagar, weeping in the wilderness, was met by the "God who sees" (Genesis 16:13).

Jonah prayed from the belly of a fish, and God caused the fish to spit him out onto dry land (Jonah 2).

In his dying moments, the thief on the cross cried out, "Remember me when You come into Your kingdom," and Jesus replied, "Today you will be with me in paradise" (Luke 23:42-43).

Blind Bartimaeus cried, "Son of David, have mercy on me!" and Jesus stopped, restored his sight, and commended his faith (Mark 10:46-52).

God's pattern is consistent. He hears. He moves. He delivers.

The Sacred Shift: From Self to Surrender

Desperation has a unique way of shifting our gaze from the self to the Savior. We can no longer rely on our strength, knowledge, or connections. We come empty, but in that emptiness, God can fill us.

As Paul writes in 2 Corinthians 12:9, "My grace is sufficient for you, for my power is made perfect in weakness." God's strength shines brightest in our weakness—our desperate, helpless state. The sacred shift occurs when we stop striving and start surrendering.

How to Seek God When You Are Desperate

Here is how to seek Him with intentionality:

Be Honest – Tell God exactly how you feel. Do not mask your emotions.

Make Time – Set aside specific prayer, worship, and Scripture reading time.

Fasting – Sacrifice something (food, media, etc.) to focus more fully on God.

Ask Boldly – Bring your requests to Him with confidence.

Listen – Do not just speak. Allow space for the Holy Spirit to respond.

Stay in Community – Let others pray with and for you.

Desperation Is Not the End—It is the Beginning

Desperation may appear as failure to you, in the eyes of the world. It is often the starting line of something new in the sight of God. The ones born in broken places are miracles. Strength rises from surrender. When focused toward God, it is desperation itself that becomes a channel of divine power.

Never forget: what you can pray at your most desperate time, can become the most remarkable testimony of your life. The night of weeping is longer than we are prepared to endure, but joy comes in the morning (Psalm 30:5).

Seek Him, not simply casually, or perfunctorily to suit for a while, all in him. He is listening to your tears; He is listening to your cries; He is listening to your silence. He is moving. Moreover, He will meet you.

The Divine Silence: When God Seems Distant

Silence is one of the most challenging aspects of seeking God in desperation. We went to prayer, crying and thirsting, even though heaven sometimes appears quiet. However, this does not feel like abandonment because oftentimes, it is a divine pause instead of a refusal.

Take, for example, the account of the story of Lazarus in John 11. Mary and Martha had sent a message to Jesus: "The one that you love is sick." Jesus did not, however, rush to Bethany. He waited two more days. Lazarus died. Hope seemed lost. However, Jesus' purpose in the delay was. He told his disciples: 'This sickness will not end in death. No, it is for God's glory so that God's Son may be glorified through it' (John 11:4). Although Jesus took a significant quantity of time to arrive, He finally did and resurrected Lazarus from the dead, much more than they had hoped.

God's silence is not absence. It tends to mean He is setting something up that we do not understand. Faith is like a seed that grows silently beneath the soil before it bursts from the surface; so does faith grow in the soil of divine silence.

Breaking Through Spiritual Barrenness

Sometimes, the crisis of desperation does not come from a crisis but from spiritual dryness. Have you ever gone through the motions of faith but not connected with the Lord? You pray, but your heart is not moved. You read the Scripture, but the words are without life. This is spiritual barrenness, one of the most desperate places for a believer.

Hannah in 1 Samuel 1 experienced this. In those days, she was faithful to God but barren year after year. Her rival provoked her. Her husband could not conceive of her pain. Before the Lord, she wept bitterly and poured out her soul. In addition, something shifted in that anguish. For she became desperate, her surrender was a prayer, and God remembered her.

Divine setup can also be a spiritual barrenness. It takes us across customary religions into untouched relationships. It impels us to cry like David, "Create in me a clean heart, O God, and renew a right spirit within me" (Psalm 51:10). If the seeking is never partially successful, God still honors that maker's first step.

Desperation in the Lives of the Early Church

The early church lived in a constant state of desperation. Under persecution, threat, and limited resources, they gathered together to pray, fast, and cry out to God. Acts 4 shows the believers praying after Peter and John were released from prison. Instead of asking for safety, they prayed for boldness. And what followed? The place where they met was shaken and filled with the Holy Spirit.

Desperation in the early church did not drive them into hiding—it launched them into mission. Their need for God's power was so real and immediate that it fueled extraordinary unity, generosity, and evangelism. This kind of desperation was not a one-time event but a lifestyle. Moreover, because of it, the Gospel spread like wildfire.

If we want to see revival today, we must embrace that same urgency. We must be willing to seek God, not just when it is convenient, but costly—through sleepless nights of intercession, sacrificial fasting, and unwavering dependence on the Holy Spirit.

The Healing Found in Surrender

Surrender is decisive; true healing, emotional healing, spiritual healing, and even physical healing often occur there. God gives healing; we tend to believe that—we look at it that way—but many times, we must be willing to grow in Christ for that healing to grow in us.

Giving up is surrender, but giving over is not. We give our timelines and deliverables to them, and they are responsible for presenting us with the desired outcomes. We pray as Jesus does in Gethsemane: 'Not my will, but yours be done' (Luke 22:42).

That night, Jesus was in the garden of Gethsemane, a garden of agony named Gethsemane. Sweat drops of blood, Jesus was in anguish. However, it was also a garden of surrender—and the most important victory the world has ever known arose from that surrender.

It is not when we figure things out that we start to heal, but when we put everything into God's hands.

Faith Beyond Feelings

In desperation, emotions run high. There can be anxiety, grief, and anger, fear swirls around or inside of us as a result. Faith is not connected to emotions, however. It is rooted in truth.

Feelings will deceive us, but faith cannot be shaken. "For by it the men of old had God testified that they were righteous; but now he testifies to us—that through faith we might obtain the promise as recipients." "Now faith is the assurance of things hoped for, the conviction of things not seen" (Hebrews 11:1, 39). God can be your peace even if you do not feel peace. You can know God is our strength when we do not feel strong.

Desperation must be directed. If left to emotions alone, it can turn into hopelessness. However, when allowed to be tethered to truth (God's unchanging Word), desperation is the soil that leads to deep, sustaining faith.

Tell your soul what the psalmist says: "Why, my soul, are you downcast?" Why am I so disturbed within myself? Trust in God" (Psalm 42:11). Preach to yourself. Speak God's promises to your pain. Moreover, choose to trust even when you cannot see the trace of His hand.

The Ministry of the Desperate

A unique calling often emerges from desperation—the call to minister to others. Those who have suffered deeply are often the ones most equipped to comfort others.

2 Corinthians 1:3-4 tells us that the "God of all comfort… comforts us in all our troubles, so that we can comfort those in any trouble with the comfort we receive from God."

Your story matters, and your healing process matters. Your journey through darkness can become a lantern for someone else. Do not despise your desperation—it might be the very thing God uses to reach others who feel unseen, unheard, and unloved.

Some of the most potent ministries are born not in seminaries but in sickbeds, prison cells, therapy rooms, and tear-soaked pillows. God uses the broken to bind up the broken.

Learning to Wait Well

It is so hard to wait, and that is desperation. Nothing changes; it challenges our patience and faith.

However, Scripture is clear: waiting is not wasted time. Then Isaiah 40:31 says, 'Those who wait on the Lord shall renew their strength'. Moreover, they shall mount up wings like eagles." Waiting is preparation. This work concerns what God carefully and deliberately does within our souls.

He spent years in prison before coming into possession. It took Abraham decades to get a promised son. Jesus started his ministry after 30 years.

Not giving up is waiting well. Such a message entails praying, serving, worshipping, and trusting. It is believing, even if the answer is not happening.

A Holy Hunger That Transforms

Desperation creates hunger, and spiritual hunger is one of the most powerful forces in a believer's life. Jesus said, "Blessed are those who hunger and thirst for righteousness, for they will be filled" (Matthew 5:6).

Hunger changes our priorities, shifts our focus, and births revival in hearts, homes, and nations. It causes us to shut off the TV and open our Bibles, gets us up at 4 a.m. to pray, and will not let us settle for surface-level religion.

When desperation ignites holy hunger, we stop being passive spectators and actively participate in God's kingdom.

Letting Desperation Lead You Deeper

Depth is the last gift of desperation. It drives us to live deeper, to go deeper than a shallow faith, to the deep waters of trust, obedience, and intimacy with God.

In Ezekiel 47, Ezekiel unnecessarily prophesies a vision of water streaming from the temple. It is ankle-deep at first, then knee-deep, then waist-deep. Eventually, it becomes a river; no one may cross it, but it is a river to swim in.

This is a desperate journey of faith. Baby steps never fail us, so we are drawn into deeper and deeper places until we have no place to stand. It is for God's Spirit to carry us now.

It is okay to let your desperation take you deeper, dig you deeper, not into despair but devotion. Do not be satisfied with ankle-deep faith for the sake of God calling you into the deep.

From Brokenness to Boldness

It is one of the most beautiful results of seeking Him in desperation. He not only restores us, but He empowers us, too. There is a way to navigate the suffering, loss, and confusion and boldly come out on the other side.

Take Peter, for example. When he was done denying Jesus three times, he was broken. He cried profoundly and probably thought that his calling was over. However, after the resurrection, Jesus did not cast him off. Peter later preached powerfully at Pentecost and led thousands to Christ, not to mention that he restored him (John 21).

This was no accidental change; he relied not on self-confidence but on the One who had shown him mercy in his lowest moment.

Your brokenness is what qualifies you, not disqualifies you. It is your training ground. God often calls the crushed to be courageous. That boldness is not a loud air of arrogance but a humble confidence in God's sufficiency.

Desperation forces us to rely on God, from whom the world's power cannot match.

Worship in the Wilderness

One of the hardest things to do in times of deep need is to worship. When everything seems to fall apart, lifting your hands or singing a song can feel impossible.

However, worship becomes a weapon in the wilderness, where provision seems scarce and comfort seems distant.

Paul and Silas, imprisoned in chains, began to sing hymns in the dead of night (Acts 16:25). Their bodies were wounded, their freedoms stripped, but their spirits soared as they worshipped. Moreover, what happened next? An earthquake shook the foundations of the prison, and every door flung open.

Worship in desperation shifts the atmosphere. It declares, "Even if I do not see the miracle yet, I trust the Miracle Worker." It confuses the enemy and strengthens the soul.

When you choose to worship in your wilderness, you invite the presence of God to reign above your pain. Moreover, in that presence, things change—sometimes externally, always internally.

Turning Desperation Into Intercession

Of course, desperation is easy to make all about ourselves. However, in mercy, God often uses pain to move others. While we are desperate for our breakthrough, we start taking on the burdens of others.

Therefore, this is intercession: praying not only on our behalf but also on behalf of those who have not yet prayed. This is standing in the gap. Selflessness is holy and was born from suffering from the flames.

Moses did this often. While the Israelites had sinned and God was ready to destroy them, Moses pleaded with God to have mercy on them (Exodus 32:11, 14). God helps us by interceding at the Father's right hand (Romans 8:34).

Desperate prayers can potentially ripple throughout your world more than your current existence. Never define yourself so low that you do not cry for yourself, your family, your community, and your country.

Intercession turns pain into purpose. It forms a bridge between your broken heart and God's heart and produces change in hidden realities.

Finding Hope in the Wait

Waiting can stretch our faith to its limits. In the waiting, doubts creep in, hope flickers, and impatience tempts us to give up or take matters into our own hands.

However, Scripture repeatedly teaches us that hope does not disappoint (Romans 5:5) because it is anchored in God's character, not our circumstances.

Abraham waited 25 years for the promise of a son, Joseph waited over a decade to fulfill his dreams, and the people of Israel waited centuries for the coming of the Messiah.

Moreover, God was still faithful. Always.

Hope is the soul's anchor (Hebrews 6:19). It grounds us when everything else feels unstable. It reminds us that delay is not denial, that God is faithful to perform what He has promised.

While you wait, speak life over your future. Hold on to His promises. Let your hope be defiant, unyielding, and firm in the face of all odds.

The Power of Honest Prayers

Desperation removes pretense. It is an invitation to be raw honesty, which allows for performance to be stripped away.

Desperate prayers are some of the most powerful prayers in the Bible (not the most eloquent). David cried, "How long, Lord? I will never forget your precepts (Psalm 119:41). Job questioned God through tears. Jeremiah wept openly. Not even Jesus had escaped the horror, crying, "My God, My God, why have You forsaken Me?" (Matthew 27:46).

These indeed were no polished prayers; furthermore, every one of them God received.

Perfect words are not necessary. You are not required to be on top of every second. Just come.

The connection between hope and despair is honest prayer. It is where healing begins. Great moments of life come from there, when you say, "God, I do not understand you, but I am still here." I still believe."

Your questions do not offend him; your sorrow does not overwhelm him. He welcomes all of it since he can see your words and heart.

Surrendering Outcomes, Trusting God's Heart

A crucial part of seeking God in desperation is learning to surrender the outcome. We come to God asking for specific things—healing, breakthrough, provision—and while it is right to ask boldly, we must also learn to trust Him even if the answer looks different from what we expected.

Shadrach, Meshach, and Abednego said it best: "Our God can deliver us… but even if He does not, we will not bow" (Daniel 3:17-18).

That is mature faith. That is the kind of faith forged in desperation and refined in surrender.

Trusting God's heart means believing He is good, even when life is not. It means resting in His sovereignty, even when the answer is "not yet" or "no."

Surrender is not passive resignation—it is active trust. It says, "God, I want Your will more than I want my own." And in that space, peace floods in.

Inviting Others Into Your Journey

We tend to isolate ourselves when we are in a state of desperation. We feel that no one will understand and are ashamed of our struggle. However, one of the most powerful things you can do in a desperate season is to invite safe, godly people into your journey.

James 5:16 supports this: "Confess your sins to one another, and pray for one another, so that you may be healed." Healing is frequently discovered not only in vertical prayer but also in horizontal connection.

You were never supposed to storm through alone. Strength, perspective, accountability, and encouragement come from the community.

Sometimes, God speaks through others when He cannot be heard directly. Sometimes, our faith is weak, but a friend carries us through.

Do not suffer in silence. Share your burden. Similarly, invite (or allow) a person to join you in prayer, crying, and walking with you. The community has healing.

The Invitation to a Deeper Walk

Desperation is not a detour; it is often the doorway from where God leads you to a deeper walk in Him. The beginning of a new level of intimacy, trust, and purpose is what it feels like at the end.

The truth is that God never wastes the desperation. He forms, molds, and brings you into a relationship with Him that does not hinge upon blessings but on intimacy with Him.

You no longer know him as your Provider, but as your Father; as your Healer, but as your Friend, your Savior, and your Shepherd.

Birth in trial, but this depth does not come in comfort. Moreover, it is priceless.

Invite this season. Do not ask God to change your circumstances, but to change you. Let Him rewrite, redefine, and restore you.

Final Reflection: Come As You Are

If you are in a season of desperation and studying all the wrongs in your life, dear reader, please hear this: you are not alone, you are seen, and you are heard. God is closer than you think.

Please do not wait to have it all figured out. It is unnecessary to wait until you feel the right occasion or consider yourself spiritually ready enough. Come as you are—broken, confused, tired, angry, and empty.

The desperate never met a door closed to them by Jesus. He drew near. He touched lepers, played with sinners, wiped tears from the poor, and gave the hopeless reason to live.

In addition, He is willing to meet you where you are at any time.

Let your desperation not make you despair, but go to the One who makes all things new.

Seek Him with thy heart. Cry out with all your soul. He is listening. Moreover, He will answer.

When You Feel Forgotten by God

In a season of desperation, there is a tranquil, significantly lingering thought that God has forgotten you. You have wept, prayed, fasted, and believed; there is a quiet. Days stretch into weeks. Hope feels fragile. You wonder whether your cries even go to heaven.

However, God's Word is true regardless of what you feel: "Can a mother forget the baby at her breast and have no compassion on the child she has borne" (Is. 49:15). If she might forget for a time, yet, I will not forget you" (Isaiah 49:15).

God does not forget you. His name is carved on the palms of His hands. He watches every tear fall, every sigh, and every whispered prayer.

Silence is not absence. Delay is not abandonment.

Moreover, He is working even when you cannot feel Him. Just as a seed grows underground in silence, before breaking the surface, that is precisely how your breakthrough grows. Stay rooted in faith. He knows the right time and will not forget you. You are deeply loved.

Learning to Lament: A Holy Expression of Grief

Many believers are desperate, and they suppress the pain for fear that it is a lack of faith. However, Scripture tells us that lamenting or grieving before God is not faithless but faithful.

There are several laments found in the Psalms. According to Psalm 42:3, 'My tears have been my bread day and night.' However, in the same psalm, David commands, 'Hope in God, for I shall again praise Him.'

Complaining is not lamenting; lament is the act of worship which says, 'God, I trust You so much I bring You my raw pain.'

Allow yourself to weep, allow your soul to sigh, let your pain find its way unto the Lord without filters or fear. He can handle it.

Lament brings healing, and grieving brings release. Honesty also means that God is closer.

Miracles in the Midnight Hour

The darkest hour is also when God's most potent interventions occur. Amid all human efforts failing, the miraculous appears when night is as long as it seems.

The Pharaoh's army was chasing the Israelites as they stood before the Red Sea. It seemed like the end. However, God split the sea to escape that moment of helplessness and terror (Exodus 14).

In Acts 12, Peter is thrown into prison and is about to be executed. However, in the middle of the night, an angel appears, the chains fall off, and he walks out free.

If you are at midnight, do not lose your heart. God is an expert at last-minute rescues, not because He is behind schedule, but so you can see that He was the One who delivered you.

Hold on. Keep watching. Moments the miracle may be away.

God of the Valleys, Not Just the Mountains

It is easy to see God in mountaintop moments when prayers are answered, joy overflows, and everything is well. But what about the valleys? The dark, low, aching places?

Scripture says, "Yea, though I walk through the valley of the shadow of death, I will fear no evil; for You are with me" (Psalm 23:4).

Your valley is not void of God. He is even more intimate in the valley. Not only is the God of the mountain, but the God of the low place.

He walks beside you in your valley. He prepares a table for you. He anoints your head with oil. Your cup will overflow—even there.

So do not fear the valley. Meet God in it.

From Surviving to Thriving: The Aftermath of Encounter

Many desperate men and women who seek God find more than relief; they find total transformation. At first, it is a matter of survival, and then it becomes revival.

Think of Hannah in 1 Samuel. In deep anguish with her, she cried out to God for a child. God did hear her, and Samuel came to be. However, that moment was answered by a prayer that became something more powerful... a ministry legacy.

When you desperately meet Him, God often gives you more than you ask. He gives you birth, ignites a calling, and gives you purpose for others.

If you become the platform that builds others, do not be surprised when the pain that broke you becomes. You are not being delivered, you are being commissioned.

God uses the healed to heal. He can walk you out of the fire free and refined.

Embracing the God Who Sees

Hagar ran away into the wilderness, bruised and abused, in Genesis 16. She was pregnant, alone, and desperate, and she sat down by the spring of water with no plan and no hope.

Besides that, the Angel of the Lord also appeared. He spoke gently, pleased her, and reassured her that there would be a future for her and her child.

Hagar named God: "El Roi" – The God who sees me, because she was overwhelmed.

You may feel unseen at the moment. However, the same God who saw Hagar sees you. Having been in your shoes, He does not just observe your situation; He understands it.

No one thanks you for the sacrifices he sees. He sees the silent battles. In obscurity, he views your faithfulness.

He is the God who sees. Additionally, He looks at us with compassion rather than with condemnation.

Letting Your Desperation Birth Intimacy, Not Just Intervention

God, they felt they could ask him for intervention, healing, provision, direction. However, sometimes induced desperation brings you to something more, to intimacy.

Sometimes, what God does in you is more significant than what He does for you.

The apostle Paul asked God to take a "thorn from his flesh." God did not remove it. He said, "My grace is sufficient for you, my power is made perfect in weakness" (2 Corinthians 12:9).

In Paul's discovery, beyond relief, was the sustaining grace that came from the intimacy of Christ.

Do not miss the invitation. If you are desperate enough, you can reach a closeness with God that comfort can never reveal.

The prayer will transition from God to God, changing this to God, be with me in this. Additionally, that closeness will give you peace that surpasses understanding.

Desperation as Preparation

What happens to be your current season may seem like a setback, but in God's hands, it is preparation.

It was not punishment for Joseph; it was preparation to be in the palace. David's wilderness did not go to waste; he trained for kingship. Jesus himself went into the wilderness prior to coming out in public ministry.

God is preparing you. He is growing endurance and character and stretching your faith.

What you are facing now is a fire that will be refined in you to prepare for what is next. Do not despise it. Embrace the process.

Eventually, one day, you will look back and comprehend that season helped put me where I was always supposed to be.

An Invitation to Surrender Daily

Desperation to seek God is not for a mere moment, but a way of life. The need for Him never ends even after the breakthrough comes.

Every day we are invited to surrender, anew, to exchange our strength for His; our plans for His will; our worry for His peace.

Desperation prompts us: this is not how life was meant to be lived without Him.

May you continually live in a surrendered posture in the daily trust, not only in crisis.

This simple prayer should act as your wake-up in the morning:

"Lord, I need You. Every hour, I need you. Lead me. Fill me. Use me."

Total dependence upon God is as safe and powerful a place as any.

Closing Prayer: The Cry of a Desperate Heart

My God, I find myself broken and desperate in the presence of this God for more than a plug-and-play quick fix, but for His presence. I give my pain, my questions, my fear. Even in the unknown, I choose to trust You. Birth faith in me, let my desperation draw me closer, not drive me away. Birth courage. Birth a deeper walk.

Be the God who sees me. Be the one who holds me. In the wilderness, I choose to worship. I think what the devil intended for evil is that you will use it for good.

Thank you for never leaving, loving me in my most debased position, and being near.

I will march into my job meetings seeking wholeheartedly, honestly, relentlessly. Moreover, I will find you. Amen.

Chapter 4: A Cry That Reached Heaven

The Divine Dialogue: Understanding the Power of Prayer

Prayer is not something we do, but a conversation between the soul, the human being, and his Creator. In it, God permits us to relate to him most personally. Prayer is not a routine conversation or a religious formality; it is raw, sincere, often unspoken, and the soul's cry. No matter whether cursed in pain, begged with faith, or shrieked in blind desperation, prayer rises above the heavens and touches the heart of God Himself.

Believers screaming out from the depths of the spirit cause things to shift in the spirit. It is not from the words polished, nor the terminology eloquent, but from the sincere humility that it does cry. Scripture assures us that God lowers His ear toward His children, especially when they pray from right standing and trust. According to James 5:16, "The effectual fervent prayer of a righteous man availeth much."

A Connection That Transcends Circumstances

Our prayer life—this, too, is an extraordinary gift from God that allows us privileged access to Him. We do not need to be in a particular place, assume a certain post, or have a specific time to pray. We can get to Him no matter if we are in the depths of a storm or the in-between moments of the day. Prayer can align us with this power that moved galaxies into formation, parted seas, healed the sick, and raised the dead.

God is not limited by where he can be or by circumstances. He met Jonah, Elijah, Daniel, and Paul in the belly of a fish, a cave, a lion's den, or prison. These accounts reflect a divine truth: God is always near and hears. The spirit of prayer is not confined by barriers that restrict our physical bodies. Heaven listens when Earth cries.

The Cry of Israel: A Nation's Deliverance

One of the most telling examples of a cry that soared to heaven is the Israelites' plight in Egypt. Slavery, beatings, oppression, and dehumanisation are what befell them. However, they responded powerfully with all the pain and suffering by crying to God.

"Exodus 2:23-25 says, The Israelites groaned in their enslavement and cried out, and their cry for help on account of their enslavement went up to God." He answered their groan and remembered His covenant... It was not a formal prayer meeting. It was not a scripted liturgy. So it was a cry from all of us, from one nation broken.

God responded.

Moses appeared to him in a burning bush. Indeed, "I have seen the misery of my people in Egypt. They have been crying out to Me... and I have been concerned about their affliction" (Exodus 3:7). Thus began one of the most amazing of David's deliverances in biblical history.

When God Appoints a Deliverer

However, God's reaction to the Israelites was very much actionable, not just emotional. Moses was appointed to be the deliverer. This message is that he is raising a solution when God hears a cry.

It is good to realise that our cries are not in vain. He hears the least of us and acts on our behalf. He sees the unseen tears and hears the silent prayers and answers in His perfect time. Sometimes, He prepares someone years ahead to answer a future prayer of someone else, as they did with Moses.

Just because we may think our prayers have been delayed doesn't mean that every cry has no answer in motion, just in God's time.

Hannah's Silent Cry: A Womb Opened by Prayer

Another tender example of divine response is Hannah's. In ancient Israel, she was barren, a place from which little or no hope sprang, a deep and culturally stigmatised pain. She reached a peak of anguish at the temple in Shiloh, where Eli, the priest, mistook her prayers for being so deep and long that they must be from liquor.

It was a wordless prayer and a powerful one. Nor did she shout or sing, but she let her soul pour out before the Lord (1 Samuel 1:15). Though silent to man, her cry was thunderous in heaven.

God promised a reply to her petition. Samuel … was one of the most influential prophets in Israel's history, and she conceived and gave birth to him. Divine transaction shows us that our cries, even the ones that are not whispers and silent words, do not go unheard. Our Father registers our anguish and answers with divine solutions.

Persistent Prayer: Jesus and the Parable of the Widow

A parable of Jesus in Luke 18:18 tells of a widow who kept troubling an unjust judge to do justice to her. In other words, she had no status, influence, or legal representation. She had persistence, but what she had was what she did. She kept coming. She kept crying. She would not be silenced.

Eventually, the judge gave her justice, not because he was righteous but because of his overindulgence in her persistence. In so doing, Jesus retold this story to show how, in faith and persistence, our loving Father in Heaven will respond even more to our cries.

"Yet will God not grant justice to His chosen ones who cry out to Him day and night?" (Luke 18:7). In this parable, we know not to give up. Even if the answers come very slowly or the sense of silence feels unbearable, we must continue to cry out. Moreover, there is no "if" in God's response but "when."

Today's Miracles: Cries That Still Reach Heaven

The truth of ancient Scripture is the same as modern testimonies; God still listens and responds. Countless people today share stories of divine intervention in moments of crisis. There are testimonies of cancer disappearing following fervent prayer, doors of finance opening despite the odds, broken marriages being restored, and the prodigal child coming home.

Ostensibly a single mother of four in a small Ugandan village, this woman kept praying for her children, asking God to provide for them. And so, with no food or income, she cried out to God and fasted. Unaware of her prayers, a Christian aid group came to her village on the seventh day, giving food supplies for the whole month. She wept, not because of the food but because Heaven had heard her.

There was a man on the edge of a suicide jump in New York City, crying one last time for God, "Are You real?" "Show me!". At that very moment, a stranger approached him, put his hand on his shoulder, and said, "You don't have to do this. God loves you." That moment was his lifesaver and lifer.

These stories are not coincidences. It was cries that went all the way to heaven.

Why Some Prayers Seem Unanswered

Why would God hear every cry if it appears specific prayers get unanswered?

Many believers have been tormented and matured by this question. God is ever responsive, but his responses are in three forms: "Yes," "Not yet," and "I have something better."

Because we are finite, we tend to read divine delays as divine denial. Isaiah 55:8-9 reminds us that 'thoughts are not your thoughts, neither are your ways My ways,' declares God. God answers prayer not for us but for him. And sometimes, something that seems like a denial is divine protection.

Crying Out in the Dark: The Power of Midnight Prayer

The Bible has many such encounters with God at nighttime. At midnight, in prison, Paul and Silas prayed and sang hymns, and their chains broke (Acts 16:25). Jacob wrestled with God throughout that night and came out with a blessing and a limp. In the early morning before dawn, Jesus often withdrew to pray.

Midnight prayer is symbolic and powerful. It is the darkest hour when it is dark and silent—hope is far, yet somehow, it is the beginning of daybreak … In spiritual terms, praying through your darkest hour can often be followed by the most significant breakthrough.

The Language of Tears

There are times when our emotions are too heavy to express in words. Yet, we do not know how or what we should pray for, as we ought. The good thing is that God knows how to read the language of tears.

Psalms 56:8: "You have taken note of my every mood." You have kept all my tears in a bottle. What have you recorded each one in your book?" It reminds us that this does not even include the measure of the tears we cry that are sacred to God. They are not wasted. Each drop is uttered in prayer, each sigh is a divine petition.

God's Response in His Time

Waiting is one of the biggest obstacles in the prayer process. These days, we want fast, instant gratification: fast food, instant downloads, real-time updates, and God's kingdom based on eternal timing.

Abraham's promise of a child waited decades before coming into fruition. Joseph spent many years locked in a prison before becoming governor. The teenage David was anointed king but waited until 30 to take the throne. God is never late. He is always on time, and His timing is perfect.

Building a Life of Consistent Prayer

Consistent prayer means living a life where our cries always go to heaven. Prayer is not for only one day; it is a lifestyle. Just like our bodies require sustenance daily, so does our spirit, which needs daily communion with God.

Having a habit of morning devotion, midday reflection, and nighttime thanksgiving allows God's presence to permeate our day. Our prayer should be like Daniel's, who, despite suffering for letting people know God and always praying three times a day, regardless, should be our non-negotiable and must-pray.

The Role of Faith in Prayer

The book of Hebrews, chapter 11, verse 6 says, "And without faith it is impossible to please God, because anyone who comes to Him must believe that He exists and that He rewards those who earnestly seek Him."

The engine of faith drives our prayer life. We believe even when we do not see the answer. And although the mountains do not seem to budge every moment, we think they will. Victory was declared before the result was seen. And when he calls those things which are not as though they were, we have in the Apostle the instance (Romans 4:17).

Encouragement for the Weary Soul

Take heart if you pray unashamedly for an extended period with no obvious answer. You are not alone. Your prayers are not in vain. You aren't suffering from delays; they are not denials. And the heavens have heard you, and your breakthrough is coming.

God is closer than you think. He is Jehovah Elohim, the God who answers; He is the God who hears (El Shama) and sees (El Roi). Your cry is precious to Him.

Keep Crying, Keep Believing

The volume of a cry that reaches heaven doesn't decide it. He hears expressed or unexpressed, long or short, happy or desperate, from the heart.

Well, so cry on, believe on, pray on. Today the same God who warding off giants, ripping open wombs, healed diseases and raised the dead is still the same, and He's listening to your cry.

If you call and answer me, I will tell you great and unsearchable things you do not know. – Jeremiah 33:3

Renewing Your Spiritual Strength Through Prayer

When life's storms and trials rage, prayer's power can renew strength. Prayer acts as a spiritual recharging, rekindling our inner being whenever our spirit is drained and the dangers of everyday activities seem weighty to carry.

The Spirit as an Oasis

See prayer as an oasis, albeit in a desert. We travelers are refreshed when we seek God's presence, just as we find our thirst quenched in an oasis. The world's noise disappears, and we are left with our Creator in all his undiluted, pure presence.

Biblical Examples of Renewal

Biblical Scripture is full of examples of renewal through prayer. David cries in the Psalms but never ceases to turn to God for renewal. "Populate my soul with fresh hope, for sake of thy name. Why so disturbed within me? Trust in God; I will praise Him yet, my Savior and my God!" (Psalm 42:5). In this, we have the struggle of despair against hope, and prayer is the solution for raising the soul from the depth of sorrow.

Embracing Restorative Practices

Steps towards renewing our spiritual strength include reserving some time daily—a few silent moments at dawn, before bed, or at some other time—to turn to prayer. These are sacred appointments with God, where you can unload your worries, pray your thanksgiving, and let Him speak such guidance as you need. Over the long run, this practice builds a relationship with God and a deep sense of inner peace and purpose.

Navigating Life's Storms with Prayer

Life comes with challenges. During trials, prayer serves as a navigation chart, a compass for the rough seas of life.

The Calm Amid the Chaos

Chaos will never shake God's truth of being our refuge and strength. During the tempest of life, our prayer is like a lighthouse offering a sure and safe harbor for the off-course ship. In moments of despair, some of us tend to lose faith in our Lord; after all, the dark forces prevail, but knowing our Lord Jeová is faithful, we can cling to the promise that our cries are heard above the storm.

Storm Narratives in Scripture

Consider the story of Jesus calming the storm (Mark 4:35-41).
Even the disciples were overtaken by fear in the presence of
howling winds and crashing waves. However, when Jesus said
this, the winds ceased, and there was great calm. This miracle
reminds us that no storm is too big to pray and believe in our
Savior. Praying in distress is one way of being a calming force.

Personal Testimonies: Weathering the Storm

Countless numbers have found comfort and solace in praying
during personal storms of their lives. They tell of a community
that a natural disaster has hit. Fear and uncertainty were
prevalent, so residents gathered for community prayer
meetings, hoping for God's intervention after prayers were laid
at the feet of the mighty God who protected and restored so
many in the aftermath and gave many a safe place to house
their souls for their remarkable recovery.

Practical Steps in the Storm

Acknowledge the Storm: Recognize your feelings and the
challenges before you. Honesty with yourself and God is the
first step in genuine prayer.

Invite Divine Presence: Pray for God's guidance and
protection. Ask Him to calm the storm, both externally and
within your heart.

Seek Support: Connect with a community of believers who
can pray with and for you, reinforcing that you are not alone on
this journey.

Reflect on Past Victories: Remember when prayer helped
you overcome adversity, strengthening your faith for the future.

Testimonies of Transformation: When Prayer Moves Mountains

Our journey through prayer is enriched by the real-life testimonies of those who have experienced miraculous change. These stories are the living proof that prayer reaches heaven and transforms lives.

The Testimony of a Healing Journey

Imagine Maria's battle with an impossible illness. The best efforts of modern medicine hadn't changed it for years. That being said, she didn't neglect prayer, spending time every day in prayer, an intimate conversation with God in which she spoke to him about whatever pain, hope and unwavering resolve she felt; just her and God. Gradually, Maria's health started to get back to what friends and family saw as a normal state: the kind of state that defied human strength, when in the blink of an eye, she went from one extreme to the other. Her symptoms ceased—if not disappeared- her vitality began to return, and doctors were astonished. Even today, Maria swears that her persistent prayer helped her recover.

A Journey from Brokenness to Wholeness

This other powerful narrative is about James, who was deeply wounded and who lost his wife to suicide. He had moments of despair, broken relationships, and they all came with an overwhelming feeling of isolation. James was overwhelmed with pain, and he turned to prayer. At first, he whispered his prayers into the void, then felt its indescribable presence. In the promises of Scripture, he began to experience inner healing and found hope in finding solace in them. Soon after, James reconciled with estranged family members, rekindled friendships, and discovered the joy of a life he hadn't heard of.

His testimony emphasises how prayer transforms what one asks for into how it heals and rebuilds the broken places.

The Ripple Effect of Answered Prayers

If prayer brings about transformation, it's not just with the individual. It spreads to families and communities and, indeed, even nations. Through worship, a single life can be transformed, and the collective attitude towards the divine can be shifted to fill others with renewed hope. Each answered prayer returned from physical ailments, repaired fractured relationships, restored financial stability, and was a collective testimony of God's enduring mercy and grace.

The Enduring Legacy of Faithful Cries

There is a profound beauty in knowing that the faithful cries of generations past continue to resonate in the halls of heaven, leaving an indelible mark on history.

Spiritual Inheritance: Lessons from the Past

Our ancestors walked paths created with faith and perseverance. Their lives of trials and triumphs offer us a rich heritage even today. A life fastened around worship in prayer has left a legacy beyond time in the prayers of Abraham, Isaac, Jacob, David, and others. God hears and responds no matter how high the walls of challenge.

Building Your Spiritual Legacy

Have a look at what regular prayer life can do for your path. Today, every prayer helps your growth and bequeaths an example for future generations. Once you share your testimony and build your trust in Christ, you are a beacon of hope unto others, a living testimony that will guide them along the way you are going.

Prayers that Change the World

History is littered with instances in which prayer has effected significant change. Communal prayers have granted communities when persecuted, nations on the edge of war, and social justice movements. This reminds humans to unite in worship to catalyse global change, breeding a spirit of unity, compassion, and divine intervention that changes the world.

Practical Ways to Deepen Your Prayer Life

This is where we must adopt the practices and disciplines to feed our love of God occasionally. In this section, you will also find practical advice that can assist you in enriching your relationship with God and transforming prayer from a routine to an enriching life habit.

Creating a Sacred Space

The first step in deepening your prayer life is creating a dedicated place for prayer, a sanctuary from your life's constant activity. This space should then incite peace and sanctity through a quiet corner of your house, a garden, or a small room allotted only for meditation and prayer. Personalise it with items of remembrance of God's love: a cross, a favorite hymn, or a few candles. This will physically represent the fact that you are willing to grow in the spirit.

Embracing a Rhythm of Prayer

Developing a rhythm in prayer means setting aside regular intervals for reflection and communication with God. Many find solace in structured prayer times, such as:

Morning Prayers: Start your day by seeking God's guidance, asking for strength, and committing your path to Him.

Midday Reflections: Take a brief pause during the day to center your thoughts, offer gratitude, or seek help with current challenges.

Evening Meditations: Conclude your day in prayer, reviewing the day's events, offering thanks, and seeking forgiveness for any shortcomings.

By incorporating these into your daily routine, you cultivate a continuous thread of divine connection that weaves throughout your day, ensuring you remain attuned to God's whisper.

The Power of Written Prayer

The following practical step is writing down your prayers. Journaling can help you sort out your thoughts, express your emotions, and record God's faithful responses over time. Consider keeping a prayer journal:

• Write down specific requests, concerns and expressions of gratitude.

• Ponder over past entries about how God has answered your prayers.

• Writing in the journal will grant insight into your spiritual journey.

Writing can mediate a slowing down and a more open heart in speaking with God.

Incorporating Different Forms of Prayer

Prayer is not a one-size-fits-all practice. Embrace various methods to connect with God:

Intercessory Prayer: Pray for yourself and others, standing in the gap for those in need.

Contemplative Prayer: Spend silence, letting God's presence fill the space around you.

Praise and Worship: Use music, art, or movement to lift your heart in joy and devotion.

Scripture Meditation: Reflect on passages from the Bible, allowing the words to speak to your soul and shape your prayer.

By exploring these different forms, you enrich your spiritual practice, making prayer a diverse and dynamic expression of your faith.

A Journey Toward Spiritual Maturity

The path of prayer is also the path towards spiritual maturity. In our growing relationship with God, we discover that worship has little to do with changing external circumstances and as much to do with changing our hearts.

Embracing the Process of Change

There is no such thing as overnight spiritual maturity. Spiritual maturity is a journey, sometimes winding, that takes place over time in small steps and profound lessons. Every prayer helps us to know who God is and to improve our character. We learn the art of surrender, humility, and patience. This process transforms our hearts into fertile soil for God's promises to grow in.

Cultivating Inner Peace

The more we spiritually grow, the more inner peace we gain, which usually makes the outer chaos less overwhelming. This inner calm is because we know we are perpetually talking with a loving God who does not care about us that much. This peace comforts us even when unsure what lies ahead and is built on consistent prayer and thought.

Lessons from the Master

Even within the demands of ministry, Jesus sought to be a witness of a Spirit-filled life by withdrawing to pray in solitude. It seems his continual communion with the Father teaches us this. He proved that it is possible through prayer always to be centered, focused, and full of divine wisdom. His example is the example that we are equipped with to be resilient to face life's challenges.

Finding Solace in Community Prayer

While personal prayer is a cornerstone of our relationship with God, communal prayer magnifies our faith and fosters an environment of mutual support.

The Strength of Fellowship

Coming together, all of us as a community of believers, is a strength. Combining many prayers creates a spiritual synergy that can sometimes unite to overcome the most difficult obstacles. Believers can share their burdens, collectively give praise for victories, and build one another up as they travel alike. Such a living proof of biblical truths that where two or three are gathered in God's name, He is there in their midst.

Examples of Communal Revival

History is replete with several revivals that were kicked off by communal prayer power. They were united in their cry towards heaven, and before long, the movements changed the course of nations and brought hope to the hopeless. Praying together unifies believers, develops an unbreakable bond, and lights the fire of righteousness through prayer groups, church congregations, and global networks.

Practical Ways to Engage in Community Prayer

Join a Prayer Group: Find or create a group in your community that meets regularly to pray for local and global concerns.

Participate in Church Services: Attend services that focus on corporate worship and prayer, where voices blend in a unified call for divine intervention.

Virtual Gatherings: In today's digital age, technology enables us to connect through online prayer meetings, transcending geographical barriers to foster a global faith community.

Embracing Hope: Prayer as a Lifelong Companion

Prayer remains a constant companion every season—guiding, comforting, and inspiring us to persevere even when the future seems uncertain.

The Unchanging Nature of God's Love

The saying is that God does not change in our lives while everything else may. His love, mercy, and power are eternal. It continues throughout life that we are never alone. God's love is unchanging; no matter our challenges, His grace is enough.

A Prayer for Every Season

In Times of Joy: Let your prayers be songs of gratitude and praise, celebrating the blessings that enrich your life.

In Times of Sorrow: Allow your tears to become prayers, trusting that God is near to comfort and console you in your grief.

In Times of Doubt: When uncertainty clouds your vision, lean on prayer as a beacon of hope that illuminates clarity.

In Times of Triumph: Even in victory, continue to offer prayers of thanksgiving, acknowledging that every success is a gift from above.

Cultivating a Heart of Gratitude

A vibrant prayer life includes gratitude in its folds. In counting blessings and remembering the countless gifts of God, we prepare our hearts to live in further revelations of His mercy. A grateful spirit is powerful and magnifies the power of prayer because you think about God's faithfulness, not the lack in the situation.

Deepening the Connection: Intercessory and Reflective Prayer

The more we confine our prayer life to asking for our personal needs and expressing deep reflection on the mysteries of faith, the richer our prayer life becomes.

The Art of Intercession

Intercessory prayer means we stand in the gap for others, bringing before God both their prayers of joy and of burden. This helps those we pray for and alters those praying. It is a source of compassion and empathy, and a way to realise how privileged it is that we are instruments of God's love.

Please think of the many biblical figures who interceded for their people. Abraham lived for Sodom; Moses begged for his nation; Jesus wept for Jerusalem. Their intercession reminds us that our prayers can change destinies, heal broken hearts, rebuild people's lives, and bring back hope.

Reflective Prayer: A Dialogue with the Inner Self

Unlike the elemental cries of the heart, the prayer of reflection is a slower, more meditative walk. In this form of worship, we are encouraged to sit quietly in God's presence and examine our thoughts, emotions, and spiritual condition. These moments of stillness are when we often receive subtle messages directing us in the right direction.

Here are some ideas to enhance reflective prayer:

Scripture Meditation: Read and ponder a passage of Scripture slowly, allowing its truths to resonate within you.

Silent Contemplation: Dedicate moments of silence where words are unnecessary, and be present before God.

Journaling Insights: After reflective prayer, write down any insights or revelations. This practice deepens your understanding and records God's guidance over time.

Bringing Prayer into Daily Action

It is not only in moments of personal transformation or when gathered communally as an action of prayer. When our prayers align with God's will, we advance toward visible displays of love, service, and justice to God.

Living Out the Faith Expressed in Prayer

Authentic prayer makes us go with our actions for our faith. When we pray for a better world, we must be told that our hands and feet must follow our hearts. Different services are offered: volunteering, listening ear, and talking to someone in need, all completed in prayer for a more compassionate society.

Prayer and Social Justice

History shows that social justice movements have prayer as their moral driving force. From the civil rights movement in America to humanitarian efforts worldwide, prayer has been the starting point for undertakings that aim to give everyone equity and dignity. When our actions align with the heart of

God's kingdom, our prayers can be for justice for the oppressed and love for those who have been marginalised.

Incorporating Prayer into Acts of Service

Make your acts of service an extension of your prayer life. Pray for the community you are about to serve initially and, in the end, reflect on the effects of your work. Invite those you serve to join in gratitude so that gratitude will ripple and spawn hope that people may share and support each other.

Building Resilience: Prayer as a Source of Strength in Adversity

When doubt or despair arises, blind faith is an unyielding pillar of strength. It's not just a routine; God's lifeline connects us to God amid life's unpredictable storms.

The Role of Prayer in Overcoming Adversity

Feeling weak or overwhelmed comes naturally in life's trials. Still, there is strength in every prayer. The apostle Paul, himself persecuted to an unbelievable extent, wrote in 2 Corinthians 12:9 that God's power is made perfect in our weakness. He acknowledged human frailty in his prayer because it opened the door for divine empowerment, and it remains true for all who cry out in need.

The Journey from Vulnerability to Victory

Persistent prayer is the path from vulnerability to victory through the fire. Every time you kneel to pray, you are reminded that you are not strong in yourself, that you are filled with a divine purpose and moved by the Creator of the universe. Every challenge presents an opportunity to see God's indistinguishable transformation of people, and every trial presents a threshold to increase faith in Him.

Drawing Courage from the Stories of the Faithful

Think about all the testimonials of individuals who received the courage to continue while in prayer. Their stories can lead us as a guide, and show us as an inspiration, to trust, whatever the darkness, that the light of divine love always wins. Nevertheless, each of those answered prayers and miraculous breakthroughs pushes it increasingly into the grand narrative of redemption that unfurls across human history.

Embracing a Lifestyle of Continuous Communication with God

Prayer should not be treated as an occasional act reserved for moments of crisis; it is a continuous, dynamic exchange that undergirds every aspect of our lives.

The Lifestyle of Unceasing Prayer

According to 1 Thessalonians 5:17, the Bible advises us to 'pray without ceasing.' Nothing in this call is a demand for a constant flow of words, but an invitation to never cease in our awareness of His presence. Each moment allows us to communicate: with the passing of thoughts, when pausing intentionally, and when pleading with passion for what is necessary.

Integrating Prayer with Everyday Moments

Picture every task and every transaction as an offering of prayer. These moments may be spent washing dishes, commuting to work, or even having a peaceful walk in nature; all are filled with the possibility of divine dialogue. You transform your day into uninterrupted worship and thanksgiving by intentionally bringing God into these ordinary moments.

The Transformative Effect on Relationships

Living a life in prayer undoubtedly transforms how we relate to others. As you develop a heart always attuned to the divine, you shine love, compassion, and understanding in every encounter. The peace you carry from your time with God allows you to listen more deeply, feel more in sync with the person, and provide authentic support. In this way, prayer changes your inner world and improves every relationship you have.

Sustaining Hope: The Endless Well of Prayer

A journey of faith, yet always in constant progression, is a well without end, burning with a fire that never dies unless the lamp is buried, nor can it be extinguished unless it is snuffed out by desperation. Because of this, even when we think we are hopeless sometimes, we are reminded that hope is never lost because we can feel that God is always listening to our prayers.

The Hope That Endures Beyond Our Understanding

Sometimes, answers appear far or concealed. In those times, if we hold onto hope, it is a strong thing to do. Our hope keeps us going and inspires us that God is working, even if the proof of it is not in front of us. It is a hope unrelated to our ability to change things but to the eternal faithfulness of our Heavenly Father.

Reflections on Hope in the Psalms

The Psalms contain the refrain of hope in adversity. Verses such as Psalm 30:5, "Weeping may endure for a night, but joy comes in the morning," assure us that the dawn of God's mercy comes after every night. In many troubles, these verses make us believe that hope is and will always be in the spirit of prayer.

Cultivating an Unbreakable Hope Through Daily Reflection

Find time every day to think about how prayer restored lightness of heart. Write down testimonies and scriptures that uplift you to create a personal anthology of divine reminders. Over time, these reflections become foundations to fortify your faith and a legacy of hope to share with others.

The Future of Your Prayer Journey

There is no ambiguity when we peer out over the ocean of our spiritual walk, as we are invited to continue feeding that relationship with God through prayer. Every day presents new opportunities to hear His voice, feel His peace, and witness the miraculous working of His fantastic plan in our lives.

Anticipating New Breakthroughs

As you are on your way, keep an expectant heart. Nothing is a closed door if the prayer is unanswered. It simply means that something infinitely greater is being arranged. May your prayer be a bridge to guide your hopes, doubts, and dreams lifelong into an ever-present God.

Sharing Your Story

An aftereffect of a prayer changed life is one of the most profound legacies you can leave behind. Converse, write, attend prayer groups, and share what you have been through with others. Perhaps your story can be a lighthouse for those amid their storm, for some cry may be out of the heavens, and their cry will not be too small to reach into the sky.

Joining the Global Chorus of Prayer

You know they are not cries; they are cries, a part of a chorus in a global church, a giant chorus of voices of faith shouting through the centuries. The prayer is joined with many others, a holy harmonising appeal to the Divine. A universal call, we never cross languages and borders to yearn for this collective thing—that in some ways, we are always looking for these connections with other people.

Final Reflections on a Lifelong Prayer Journey

Remember, then, these other reflections that were added, that prayer is a long journey of relentless hope, continual renewal, and deep connection with God that changes us. The lessons in these sections are not unique but intermingled with other lessons, weaving into the rich tapestry of our spiritual lives.

Embracing the Fullness of Prayer

Learn from each moment of prayer about the endless love of the Creator. Learn to rejoice in every whisper of wind on a day with no other sound, in a silent pause when silence speaks, and in any stir of the heart. Here in this fullness, we see our lives as signs of God's grace, each prayer an eternal verse of redemption.

A Call to Endurance and Grace

May these words encourage you in the things that lie ahead, even when the journey extends long and the night is dark. Each cry that ascends to heaven requires an answer that answers to a purpose of a divine order far above what we can conceive. Beware of this truth with the spirit of endurance and grace, knowing that each conversation with God always adds to your life.

Continuing the Journey

However, the adventure of prayer has to start. It becomes an ever-expanding dialogue that is growing richer and richer, and day by day, it does grow richer. May you continue to walk the road of discovering deeper waters of worship and never lose hope while having strength and a sense of belonging in the loving presence of the Divine.

May the prayer journey be your lamp unto them; a companion in every season of one's life. With every heartfelt cry, you add to the legacy of faith, hope, and divine love that will reach without end in nature and eternity. Whether or not you are there or which burdens you must deal with, you will always have an unending love, an unshakeable hope, and a grace that never fails.

May your way be walked with a zillion encounters and conversations with God—each prayer moves you one step closer toward the God who can hear you, care for you beyond imagination, and interrupt our souls' deepest darkness in unimaginable ways.

Moreover, the deeper you go into the depths of prayer upon a lifelong journey, the more intimate and abiding it is, affecting your communion with the heart of heaven. Every prayer, uttered in silence or the company of other believers, is proof that faith can carry on. Keep believing and crying; keep the doors of your heart open for the unsearchable wonders to be discovered in the life of prayer.

An extended reflection on the virtue of prayer with helpful practical guidance, personal testimonies, and copious encouragement is a testimony to the power of prayer. This journey has no end, and it's as beautiful, intimate, grand, and eternal as God's love.

Chapter 5: Walking with God Through the Storm

Being a faith follower means embracing a journey that does not always make logical sense. It is not a path laid out in a straight line or a predictable formula that yields immediate results. By its very nature, faith defies strict reasoning and calls us into a relationship of continual trust, patience, and endurance. It is a dynamic and evolving process, a daily walk with the Divine through calm and storm.

The Reality of Faith in Crisis

Faith is easy when the skies are blue, our prayers are swiftly answered, and blessings overflow. However, true faith—the kind that sustains and transforms—is tested in the furnace of adversity. When darkness descends and our plans unravel, we must decide whether to trust God even when we cannot trace His hand. In these moments, our trust becomes an anchor.

Jesus Himself prepared us for this reality. In John 16:33, He says, "In this world you will have trouble. But take heart! I have overcome the world." These words are not just a warning but a comfort. They acknowledge the inevitable trials while offering the assurance of victory through Christ. The context of this verse is Jesus' farewell discourse to his disciples, where he prepares them for the challenges they will face after his departure. It does not matter if storms will come, but when and how we respond.

Anchored in the Storm

The storms of life can take many forms: financial hardship, illness, broken relationships, mental anguish, and spiritual doubt. Each storm carries its weight and threat. However, Scripture assures us that we are not alone. Psalm 46:1 declares,

"God is our refuge and strength, an ever-present help in trouble." This verse does not promise exemption from trouble; it promises God's presence within it.

Peter's Leap of Faith

One of the most vivid portrayals of faith amid chaos is found in Matthew 14:29-31. At Jesus' command, Peter exits the boat and walks on water. He does the impossible as long as his eyes are fixed on Jesus. However, the moment he becomes distracted by the wind and the waves, fear overtakes him, and he begins to sink. Still, even in his doubt, Peter cries out, "Lord, save me!" Moreover, immediately, Jesus reaches out His hand.

This narrative teaches us that storms are not the enemy—fear and distraction are. When we shift our focus from Christ to the chaos, we falter. However, when we cry out in desperation and faith, Jesus will always lift us. This moment encapsulates the entire Christian walk: taking bold steps of faith, stumbling, and being caught by grace.

Faith Refined by Fire

Trials are not just unfortunate detours in life—they are integral to spiritual maturity. James 1:2–4 advises us to "consider it pure joy... whenever you face trials of many kinds, because you know that the testing of your faith produces perseverance." The testing process is not punitive; it is redemptive. Like gold refined in the fire, our faith emerges stronger, purer, and more resilient.

When we go through the storms, our character is shaped, our perspective deepens, and our dependence on God intensifies. The pain we experience is not wasted. Romans 5:3-5 explains that suffering produces perseverance; perseverance, character; and character, hope. Moreover, hope does not disappoint.

Surrendering Control

Trusting God often requires surrender. We must let go of the need to control outcomes, know every detail, and foresee every twist in the road. Romans 8:28 assures us that "in all things God works for the good of those who love Him." That includes the things that hurt, confuse, and frustrate us.

As 2 Corinthians 5:7 instructs, walking by faith means moving forward even when the path is obscured. It means choosing trust over fear, obedience over comfort, and surrender over self-reliance. In our surrender, we find strength, because we no longer rely on ourselves but on the One who holds all things together.

Resting in God's Promises

The promises of God are the foundation upon which we build our lives. Hebrews 10:23 encourages us to "hold unswervingly to the hope we profess, for He who promised is faithful." God's faithfulness does not depend on our circumstances; it is rooted in His unchanging nature. This unyielding faithfulness is our anchor in the storm, a source of security and hope that He will never leave or forsake us.

Sometimes, His silence feels like absence, and His delays feel like denials. However, we are called to remember who He is and what He has already done in those seasons. The same God who parted the Red Sea, shut the mouths of lions, and raised the dead is the One who walks with us today.

Testimonies from the Storm

Throughout history and within our communities, testimonies abound of those who have walked through storms and emerged with a deeper faith. Consider the story of Horatio Spafford, who penned the hymn "It Is Well with My Soul" after losing his children in a tragic shipwreck. His words, born out of unimaginable grief, inspire millions today. His storm did not break him; it refined him.

Likewise, contemporary believers facing cancer, job loss, or depression have testified to the nearness of God in their suffering. Their stories are not fairy tales of instant deliverance but chronicles of enduring faith. These witnesses remind us that storms may shape us, but do not have to shatter us.

Enduring Through Community

One of the greatest gifts God gives us during storms is the presence of others. Galatians 6:2 exhorts us to "carry each other's burdens, and in this way you will fulfill the law of Christ." The Christian walk is not a solo journey. We are called to walk alongside others, offering encouragement, prayer, and tangible support. This community support is a lifeline and a source of strength and upliftment amid trials.

In times of trial, the community becomes a lifeline. A phone call, a prayer circle, a meal, or a word of encouragement can be the very means God uses to strengthen a weary soul. When we share our struggles, we allow others to be vessels of God's grace, fostering a sense of unity and shared burden.

Cultivating a Storm-Proof Faith

Faith that endures the storm does not happen by accident. It must be cultivated through regular spiritual practices: prayer, worship, Scripture meditation, and obedience. These disciplines deepen our intimacy with God and anchor us when the winds begin to howl. They are not just routines, but powerful tools that empower us to face the storms of life with a firm and unshakable faith, giving us the strength and resilience to weather any storm.

Daily time in the Word renews our minds and reinforces God's truth. Persistent prayer draws us into God's presence and aligns our will with His. Worship shifts our focus from our problems to God's power. Obedience, even when it is hard, strengthens our spiritual muscles. Each of these practices fortifies us for the storms ahead.

Eyes on Jesus

Ultimately, the key to walking with God through the storm is keeping our eyes on Jesus. Hebrews 12:2 tells us to "fix our eyes on Jesus, the author and perfecter of our faith." He is our example, our sustainer, and our Savior. When we look to Him, we find courage. When we listen to Him, we find direction. When we trust Him, we find peace.

Life will never be free from storms. However, as long as we walk with Jesus, we will never walk alone. His presence is our peace, His Word our anchor, and His love our shelter.

The Storm is Not the End

Every storm has a beginning, a middle, and—praise God—an end. It may feel eternal while you are in it, but it is temporary. Even the fiercest hurricanes eventually lose strength. So it is with spiritual battles. 2 Corinthians 4:17 tells us, "For our light and momentary troubles are achieving for us an eternal glory that far outweighs them all."

That "eternal glory" does not just begin in heaven. It starts the moment we walk by faith, hand in hand with the Lord. We walk into glory whenever we choose to trust instead of fear, praise instead of complain, and keep moving instead of giving up.

Storms are seasons, not destinies. Weeping may endure for a night, but joy comes in the morning (Psalm 30:5). You may feel buried right now, but perhaps God is planting you for a greater harvest.

God's Sovereignty in the Storm

One of the most powerful truths to embrace in the storm is this: God is sovereign. He is not surprised by what you are facing. He is not scrambling for a Plan B. God reigns, even when the earth shakes beneath your feet.

In Genesis 50:20, Joseph tells his brothers, "What you intended for harm, God intended for good." That is the lens through which every believer must learn to see suffering. God does not cause all storms, but He permits them and always uses them. His sovereignty means He can take what the enemy meant for evil and turn it into the soil that produces fruit in your life.

When you trust God's sovereignty, you stop needing all the answers. You rest in the One who holds the blueprint, even when all you can see are the broken pieces.

Rebuilding After the Storm

Walking with God through the storm is one thing—rebuilding after it is another. Sometimes, the storm takes stuff with it—relationships, careers, health, dreams. Moreover, while the storm may pass, the aftermath remains.

However, God is a Master Restorer.

In Joel 2:25, He promises, "I will restore to you the years that the locust has eaten." He does not just repair—He restores. That means He can bring back more than what was lost. The Lord specializes in redemption. What was once desolate can bloom again.

Rebuilding requires patience and partnership. God will lay the foundation, but you must pick up the bricks. It is in this process that trust deepens and wisdom grows. The wounds may remain as scars, but even scars can become testimonies of healing.

The Gift of Perspective

Storms teach us to see differently. They rearrange our priorities. Things we once considered urgent lose importance, while the eternal becomes essential.

In the storm, God adjusts our spiritual lenses. We begin to value His voice over the crowd's approval. We learn the preciousness of peace, the necessity of prayer, and the sweetness of His presence.

Sometimes, the storm is not meant to destroy us—it is intended to deliver us from idols, distractions, or patterns quietly destroying us from within.

As C.S. Lewis said, *"God whispers to us in our pleasures, speaks in our conscience, but shouts in our pains. It is His megaphone to rouse a deaf world."*

The perspective we gain in storms cannot be learned in comfort. It must be lived.

When the Storm Returns

Some storms are seasonal. Others revisit like uninvited guests. When you feel like you have recovered, another wave hits. If this is you, take heart. You are not failing. You are fighting.

Even Paul, a spiritual giant, wrote in 2 Corinthians 12:7-10 about a "thorn in the flesh" that remained despite his repeated prayers. God did not remove it but gave Paul something better: "My grace is sufficient for you, for My power is made perfect in weakness."

The repetition of the storm is not a sign that you are abandoned—it is often a sign that you are being strengthened for sustained spiritual impact. Every return is a chance to deepen dependence on God and trust that His grace will carry you again.

Raising a Hallelujah in the Storm

Praise is not a reaction to peace but a weapon in the storm. When all seems lost, worship is one of a believer's most potent acts. It confuses the enemy and releases a breakthrough in the spirit realm.

Acts 16:25-26 tells us that Paul and Silas, while in prison, sang praises at midnight. Not only did their chains break, but everyone's chains broke. That is the power of praise in the storm. It does not just liberate you—it can set others free.

Raise a hallelujah, even if your voice trembles. Sing when there is nothing left. Your song becomes a declaration: *My God is greater than this.*

Walking Others Through Their Storms

Once you have weathered your storm, you are uniquely positioned to walk others through theirs. Do not waste what you have endured—redeem it.

2 Corinthians 1:3-4 says that the God of all comfort comforts us in our troubles so that we may comfort others with the same comfort we have received.

Your testimony may be the roadmap someone else needs. Your scars may be the proof someone else clings to. There is power in saying, *"I have been there, and He brought me through."*

Let your life be a lighthouse. Let your story illuminate hope for others sailing through the dark.

The Storm and the Kingdom

Storms are not just personal—they have Kingdom implications. How we walk through them shapes our witness to the world. When unbelievers see peace in us amid chaos, they ask, *"What do you have that I do not?"*

This is your moment to shine—not through perfection but through authentic trust in Jesus. When we allow the Spirit to shape us in the storm, we become ambassadors of the unshakable Kingdom.

Hebrews 12:28 says, "We are receiving a Kingdom that cannot be shaken." That is what we carry, even in the storm. Moreover, that is why, in the face of disaster, we do not collapse—we rise.

Strengthening the Inner Man

Storms have a way of revealing the condition of our inner man—our spiritual core. When everything around us is stripped away, what remains inside becomes evident. This is where God does His most intimate work.

Paul prayed in Ephesians 3:16, "That He would grant you, according to the riches of His glory, to be strengthened with might through His Spirit in the inner man." This strengthening Is not surface-level encouragement. It is divine reinforcement from within—resilience that does not come from personality but presence.

When the outer man is overwhelmed, the inner man can still stand tall, because the Spirit of God resides there. If your outer world is collapsing, let God deepen your inner world. Your weapons are stillness, meditation on Scripture, and prayer in the Spirit.

Spiritual endurance is not about ignoring pain but being empowered to endure it purposefully.

Discernment amid the Tempest

One of the most significant challenges in spiritual storms is discernment—knowing what is from God, what is an attack, and what is simply life in a fallen world.

The enemy thrives in confusion, but God gives us clarity.

Hebrews 5:14 tells us that mature believers have "their senses exercised to discern both good and evil." "Exercised" implies training—it is developed, not instant. The storm becomes a classroom for discernment. As we press into God's Word and His Spirit, we recognize His voice in the chaos.

Sometimes, the storm is God's way of repositioning you. Other times, it is the enemy trying to derail your destiny. Discernment helps you know when to speak peace to the storm and when to ride it out in obedience. Without discernment, we risk fighting the wrong battles—or worse, resisting God's pruning.

The Hidden Oil of the Pressing

Every believer desires the anointing, but few understand how it is produced. It does not fall from the sky. It is pressed from the crushing.

In the ancient world, oil came from olives crushed under intense weight. Likewise, spiritual authority and power often emerge from seasons of deep pressure. In Gethsemane—literally "the place of the oil press"—Jesus prayed until His sweat became like drops of blood.

There is oil in your crushing.

When you emerge from the storm with more profound compassion, fresh revelation, and undeniable faith, you carry oil. This oil heals the broken, casts out darkness, and shifts atmospheres. The anointing breaks the yoke (Isaiah 10:27), but it is birthed in the secret places of pain.

Do not resent the pressing. Embrace it as the sacred process of becoming more like Christ.

Prophetic Clarity Through Suffering

Storms often strip away the noise of life, sharpening our spiritual sight. In quiet desperation, we hear God more clearly. Like Elijah in the cave, we learn that God is not always in the wind, the fire, or the earthquake—but in the still, small voice (1 Kings 19:12).

Prophetic insight does not always come on mountaintops. It often comes in valleys. God speaks deepest when our souls are most quieted. Suffering clears space in our spirit. What once distracted us now feels irrelevant. What once satisfied no longer does. This sanctified focus becomes fertile ground for vision.

Many of God's prophets were trained in obscurity and pain. Moses had the wilderness, Joseph had the pit and prison, and David had the caves. Moreover, God spoke.

If you feel like you are in the storm alone, listen. The voice of God is nearer than you know. He speaks in storms not just to comfort, but to commission.

Healing the Identity Crisis After the Storm

One of the most subtle consequences of a prolonged storm is the distortion of identity. When everything is shaken—job, ministry, relationships—there is a temptation to believe the lie that your value is tied to what you have lost.

However, identity in the Kingdom is not performance-based—it is presence-based. You are who God says you are, not what the storm took from you.

Jesus' identity was affirmed before He did a miracle: "This is My beloved Son, in whom I am well pleased" (Matthew 3:17). The Father speaks the same affirmation over you, especially when you feel least deserving.

The enemy will try to rename you in the storm: *"Failure." "Forgotten." "Unworthy."* However, heaven still calls you: *"Beloved." "Redeemed." "More than a conqueror."*

Healing after the storm must include restoring one's true identity—not just what one does but who one is in Christ.

The Legacy of Faith Built in Storms

Faith that has been tested is faith that leaves a legacy. What you walk through now becomes the foundation someone else will stand on. That's Kingdom multiplication.

Hebrews 11 is filled with heroes who endured great storms—but it is not just a list of names; it is a testimony of what faith looks like in real life. Storms produce stories that generations need to hear.

Your children will see how you endured, your spiritual sons and daughters will lean on your wisdom, and your authenticity will edify the church. Heaven will take note when you stay faithful in the fire.

When you trust God in the dark, you build more than survival—you establish a spiritual inheritance that will outlive you.

Angels in the Storm

The unseen realm is never more active than when a child of God is enduring a storm. Psalm 91:11 assures us, *"For He shall give His angels charge over you, to keep you in all your ways."* This is not a poetic metaphor—it is divine reality.

Angels are not just for supernatural encounters or distant Bible stories. They are ministering spirits, sent to assist heirs of salvation (Hebrews 1:14). When the storm rages fiercest, heaven deploys reinforcements.

Think of Peter, locked in prison and bound with chains—yet an angel awakened him and led him past guards and locked gates (Acts 12:6-11). The storm was real, but so was the angelic intervention.

You may not always see them, but you are never outnumbered. The Kingdom does not panic when the earth shakes—heaven mobilizes. Angels encamp around those who fear the Lord (Psalm 34:7). Even in your darkest hour, angelic hosts surround you. Sometimes their work is quiet; sometimes it is dramatic. However, they are always on assignment.

You are not alone in this battle. Divine backup has already been dispatched.

Rebuilding with Holy Precision

After the storm subsides, many believers look at the wreckage and wonder, *"What now?"* This is where divine wisdom must take the lead. Rebuilding is not just about recovery—it is about reformation.

God never wastes a storm. He allows it to tear down what was fragile or misaligned so He can rebuild according to His heavenly blueprint.

In Nehemiah 2:18, after hearing of Jerusalem's broken walls, Nehemiah declared: *"Let us rise and build."* Moreover, they did—with prayer, strategy, and tools in one hand and weapons in the other.

Your rebuilding season will require both. You will need spiritual discernment to avoid recreating the past. God does not want to restore you to what you had, but to what He intended.

This means carefully laying new foundations, prioritizing intimacy over performance, obedience over ambition, and surrender over control.

Let the Spirit lead the blueprint. Build with holy precision.

Worship as Warfare

Storms often silence believers. However, God is raising a generation who know how to worship in warfare. Not worship as a reaction, but worship as a weapon.

In 2 Chronicles 20, King Jehoshaphat faced a massive army. However, instead of sending soldiers first, he sent singers: "Give thanks to the Lord, for His mercy endures forever." As they worshipped, the enemy turned on itself.

Worship is not denial—it is defiance. It declares: *"Though I walk through the valley of the shadow of death, I will fear no evil."* It shifts atmospheres, shakes prisons (Acts 16), and silences the enemy.

Ask the Spirit to restore your song if you have lost your song in the storm. Sing even when it hurts. Praise even when it is quiet. Your worship is prophetic—it tells hell that it did not win.

Do not wait for deliverance to worship—worship until deliverance breaks in.

Community in Crisis

Isolation is one of the enemy's most effective tools. If he can separate you from the Body of Christ, he can weaken your resistance. However, in the Kingdom, we are not meant to stand alone.

Even Jesus, in His most painful moment, invited Peter, James, and John to "watch and pray" with Him in Gethsemane. Matthew 26:38 records His words: *"My soul is exceedingly sorrowful, even to death. Stay here and watch with me."*

Storms are not meant to be endured in silence. We need people who will weep with us, war with us, and wait with us.

In Galatians 6:2, Paul exhorts: *"Bear one another's burdens, and so fulfill the law of Christ."* That word "burden" means an overwhelming weight—something one cannot carry alone.

Do not suffer in isolation. The Body is designed to be a shelter in the storm. Find your tribe. Let them hold you up. Moreover, I want to be the one who holds others up, too.

God of the Aftermath

When the winds have stopped and the waters recede, you might look around and think, *"I am not the same person anymore."* That is true. You are not.

Storms are transformative. You come out marked—sometimes with scars, always with wisdom. The version of you that emerges is not broken, but refined.

Job 23:10 says, *"But He knows the way that I take; when He has tested me, I shall come forth as gold."* Gold does not fear the fire because it knows its value increases through it.

The God who allowed the storm is the same One who walks you through the wreckage. He does not just restore—He redeems. He multiplies what was lost. He breathes life into dry bones. He causes all things to work together for good (Romans 8:28).

Let Him guide your steps in the aftermath. There is a promise on the other side of pain. Moreover, He is faithful in bringing beauty from ashes.

The Mantle Gained in the Storm

Spiritual storms are not just battles—they are transitions. Elijah's stormy encounter with God on Mount Horeb led to his passing of his prophetic mantle to Elisha.

Likewise, the storm you are enduring may be the birthplace of a new mantle.

Mantles in Scripture symbolize spiritual authority, calling, and assignment. Moreover, they are often bestowed in moments of deep vulnerability and transition. You do not earn them through status—you receive them through surrender.

Some mantles come after you have been crushed. Others go after you have wept on your knees, clinging to the altar. However, make no mistake—your storm may be the gateway to your next level in the Spirit.

Do not despise the shaking. It may be the very thing making room for your next anointing.

The Storm and the Seed

What if your storm is not a grave, but a garden?

In John 12:24, Jesus said, *"Unless a grain of wheat falls into the ground and dies, it remains alone; but if it dies, it produces much grain."*

Sometimes, storms feel like a burial. However, God sees them as planting.

You have been sown in tears but will reap in joy (Psalm 126:5). Every lost dream, broken plan, and surrendered desire is a seed in God's soil. Moreover, He is not unjust in forgetting what you have laid down.

What you thought died in the storm will break through the surface with new life, purpose, and fruitfulness. However, do not rush the process. Seeds grow in darkness, below the surface, away from human eyes.

Your storm is not the end. It is the beginning of a harvest you cannot yet see.

The Oil That Only Flows Under Pressure

Anointing does not come cheap. While we often celebrate anointed preaching, healing, or breakthrough, we rarely see the crushing that produced it. Like olives, we must be pressed to release oil, so we must be pushed to release anointing.

In 2 Corinthians 4:8-9, Paul writes: *"We are hard-pressed on every side, yet not crushed... struck down, but not destroyed."* Why? Because what is in us is greater than what surrounds us. Moreover, when pressure hits, the Spirit within us flows.

Jesus Himself was crushed in Gethsemane—literally meaning "oil press." Moreover, under the weight of sorrow and obedience in that garden, His purpose moved from preparation to fulfillment.

Your storm is producing oil.

Not the kind that impresses crowds—but the kind that breaks yokes. The kind that flows in hospital rooms, board meetings, prison cells, and pulpits alike. Oil that smells like sacrifice, prayer, and perseverance.

Do not curse the pressure. Embrace it. Because the greater the crushing, the purer the oil.

When the Storm Is Inside You

Not all storms are visible. Some rage within the soul—silent battles that never make it to prayer requests or social media updates. These are the internal storms: the ones that attack your identity, erode your confidence, and whisper lies when the world is silent.

David understood this storm well. In **Psalm 42:11**, he cries, *"Why, my soul, are you downcast? Why am I so disturbed within myself? Put your hope in God..."* Here, the man after God's own heart speaks directly to his soul. He did not deny the storm inside—he confronted it.

Sometimes the greatest spiritual warfare is not with demons or systems, but with our thoughts.

The enemy's fiercest weapon is suggestion: *"You are not enough." "God is not listening." "This will not end."* When those lies take root, they create emotional hurricanes that spin out of control.

However, here is the truth: even in your internal chaos, **God is still God.** His love is not based on your mood; your confusion does not cancel his promises. You can speak to your soul, just as David did, and command it to *hope again.*

Internal Storm Survival Strategies:

Renew your mind daily (Romans 12:2) with Scripture.

Practice honest prayer. God can handle your anxiety, doubts, and fear.

Choose worship over worry. Worship shifts the atmosphere within you.

Refuse isolation. Reach out to the community—even when you feel unworthy.

When the storm is inside, you must lean harder on the God who lives within. Greater is He that is **in you** than any wave that crashes against you (1 John 4:4).

The Blessing Hidden in the Battle

One of the most frustrating realities of walking with God is that His blessings often come disguised as battles. Many things you are praying against might be the pathway to what you have been praying for.

Let us revisit Joseph. Sold into slavery. Betrayed. Imprisoned. Forgotten. However, every painful step was a promotion in disguise. **Genesis 50:20** gives us the key to understanding this storm: *"You intended to harm me, but God intended it for good..."*

This is divine reversal.

God is not surprised by your storm. He may have orchestrated it not to destroy you, but to deliver you to a place of greater authority, wisdom, and usefulness.

The battle is proof of the blessing.

You would not be under attack if there were nothing inside you worth fighting for. Casual Christians do not threaten the devil. However, a believer who prays through storms? That is a threat to darkness.

What if your pain is the womb of your next ministry?

What if your tears are watering the seeds of a harvest you cannot yet see?

Blessings do not always come with bows. Sometimes they come with bruises. However, if you endure, they always arrive.

Breaking Generational Storms

Not all storms start with us. Some are inherited. Spiritual, emotional, and behavioral patterns passed down through generations—addiction, anxiety, abuse, poverty, shame. These storms are fierce because they feel like destiny.

However, hear this: in Christ, **you are the storm breaker.**

The blood of Jesus is not just for forgiveness—it is for **freedom.** Moreover, that includes the freedom to rewrite the story of your family.

Isaiah 61:4 speaks of those who will *"rebuild the ancient ruins and restore the places long devastated."* That is you.

You were born again to stand in the gap and say, "The dysfunction stops with me."

Storm breakers:

- Renounce family curses and claim Christ's identity.
- Pray strategically and specifically, calling out every pattern.
- Live differently and intentionally, even when it is hard.
- Raise your children in truth, peace, and power.
- Your obedience today becomes someone else's freedom tomorrow.
- Storms that lasted for generations can be silenced in **your lifetime**.

When God Uses the Storm to Speak

Sometimes, we ask God to end the storm, but God's goal is not to stop it but to **speak through it.**

In **1 Kings 19**, the prophet Elijah is running. He is afraid, exhausted, and hiding in a cave. He wants God to show up in a fire or an earthquake, but God shows up in a *whisper.*

Why?

Because when you are in a storm, **you are listening differently.** Pain tunes your ears to frequencies of heaven that comfort never could.

God speaks in the storm:

To clarify your purpose (He reminded Elijah of his assignment).

To realign your heart (He rebuked fear and affirmed identity).

To release new instructions (He sent Elijah to anoint new leaders).

Do not just ask, "When will this be over?" Ask, "What are you saying, Lord?"

When God speaks in storms, He is not wasting words. He is setting the course for your **next season.**

Still Standing

Let us be honest. Some storms do not end the way we want. We lose people. We do not get the miracle. We still carry scars. However, here is the miracle most people overlook:

You are still standing.

Ephesians 6:13 says, *"…and after you have done everything, to stand."* Not to impress, perform, or even conquer—to **stand.**

You survived what should have shattered you. You did not curse God. You did not walk away. You held on. Moreover, maybe it was not pretty, but you are still here. That is a victory.

Standing is faith. Standing is worship. Standing is warfare.

Every scar you carry is a **testimony**, not of weakness, but of endurance. Of God's grace. Of your identity as an **overcomer.**

Do not underestimate the power of standing.

Conclusion: Anchored in the Eye of the Storm

Storms reveal what is beneath the surface, not just in the skies, but in us. They shake loose illusions, uproot idols, and strip away everything that is not eternal. In many ways, the storms of life, though unwanted, are sacred places. In them, we come face to face with our fragility. However, more importantly, we come face to face with our **Father**.

From the pages of Scripture to the everyday lives of believers, one thing becomes clear: storms are not signs of God's absence—they are invitations into His **presence**. They teach us not just how to survive, but how to walk with God more deeply, humbly, and courageously.

Let us take this time to reflect on everything we have seen, heard, and learned throughout this chapter. Not just as theory, but as life-truths—soul anchors—that will steady us when the winds rage again. Because they will.

The God Who Walks Into Our Storms

One immutable truth lies at the heart of this journey: **Jesus enters storms**. He does not watch from a distance nor delegate comfort to angels. He walks on the waves themselves. He calms the seas, but sometimes He climbs in the boat with us.

When Peter cried out, "Lord, save me!" the response was immediate, not delayed, not after a lecture, not based on performance. However, **immediate grace**—a hand stretched through the storm to a drowning disciple.

This is who He is—a God who does not wait for us to swim out of trouble but reaches into it with us. If Peter's moment tells us anything, God is not intimidated by the mess we make in the middle of our faith journey. He rescues, restores, and repositions us, not based on perfection but on relationship.

Jesus did not ask Peter, "Why didn't you swim better?" He asked, "Why did you doubt?" That is the divine diagnosis of sinking souls: **not lack of ability, but misplacement of trust**.

If we learn nothing else, let us cling to this: **keep your eyes on Jesus.** When we look at the waves, fear wins. When we look at the Savior, faith rises.

The Refining Fire of Trials

We also cannot forget what James 1 taught us: *"Consider it pure joy when you face trials..."* This command feels radical because it is. Who welcomes pain? Who sings of suffering?

However, joy in trials is not about denial but about being deeply rooted in a reality that surpasses what we see. It is the assurance that every storm, no matter how dark, **is under the sovereign hand of God.** He is not the author of evil but the Master of redemption.

Trials refine us. They burn off what we do not need. They separate the shallow from the sincere. Faith that has not been tested is still theory. However, once it walks through fire and still believes, it becomes a **testimony**—an unshakable evidence that God is honest, faithful, and able.

The trial that once felt like a tomb can become the very womb of your calling. You are not just surviving. You are **becoming.**

The Testimony of Stillness

So much of our modern faith is fast and loud. However, often, God's voice is most unmistakable in stillness. That is why He met Elijah in a whisper, not fire, wind, or quakes. Sometimes, the storm outside forces us to silence the noise within.

Stillness is not passivity. It is a spiritual **stance**—a declaration that *"God is my refuge. I will not be moved."* Psalm 46:10 urges us to *"Be still and know that I am God."* Stillness is the sacred space where revelation is born.

We are not just waiting but worshiping when we remain in a storm. We are declaring trust in God's timing, plan, and sovereignty. Moreover, this trust is not naive—it is **warfare.**

The enemy wants you to be anxious. He wants you to be reactive. However, God calls you to a higher place: the shelter of the Most High, where peace does not depend on circumstances but on **presence.**

Legacy Carved in the Storm

We also explored how some storms are not ours alone but part of generational patterns. You did not choose the trauma. You did not start the dysfunction. However, **you can stop it.**

Storm-breakers are often forged in the fire of their pain. They are the first in their family to walk in purity, peace, or purpose. They carry wounds, yes—but also weapons. They are the answer to the prayers of ancestors who never knew freedom.

What you conquer now creates paths for those who come after. Your children will not have to fight every battle you fought— because you fought it first. You set the standard. You changed the tide.

This is not just about personal peace. It is about the **kingdom's legacy.** The storm you endure may be the foundation upon which your family's future is built.

The Warrior Who Worships

One of the most radical truths in Scripture is that **worship is warfare**. When you praise God in the middle of your pain, heaven moves.

Paul and Silas proved this in Acts 16. In chains, beaten, bloodied—they sang. Moreover, the earth responded. Chains broke. Doors opened. And not just for them, but for every prisoner around them.

Your worship in the storm is not just for you. It liberates others. It proclaims to every principality and power that **God is still worthy,** no matter what you are going through.

You do not need perfect pitch. You need **persistent praise.**

Do not wait for the storm to pass. **Sing now.** Cry if you must. Kneel if you are tired. However, **do not stop worshiping because** worship is how we win, even when we are weak.

The Mystery of Unanswered Prayers

There is another kind of storm: the kind that lingers. The kind where we pray, fast, believe, and still do not see the outcome we hoped for. The healing does not come. The door does not open. The pain does not lift.

These are the deepest valleys. However, even here, God is faithful. Sometimes, His most incredible mercy is not in removing pain but in the gift of **His presence in the middle of it.**

Paul asked God three times to remove his thorn. God did not. But He answered with this: *"My grace is sufficient for you, for My power is made perfect in weakness."* (2 Corinthians 12:9)

Not every storm ends the way we wish. However, God's grace carries us through **every storm.** His grace fills the cracks, holds us upright when we have no strength left, and transforms what should have been a grave into a platform for His glory.

When God says no, He is not rejecting us. He is **redirecting** us into a deeper dependence on Him.

Moreover, sometimes, the very storm that seemed like a curse becomes the doorway into a level of intimacy with God we never would have discovered otherwise.

Still Anchored, Still Here

Let us not tie it with a perfect bow as this chapter draws close. Life is not neat. Faith is not sterile. Storms are messy.

However, the truth binds everything together: **God never wastes a storm.**

He uses every wave, every wind, every tear, every night of silence, every morning of new mercy—to write His story in your life—a story not of easy faith, but of **enduring faith.**

You are not disqualified because you struggled, weak because you wept, or less holy because you asked, "Why?"

You are human.

However, more than that, you are a **child of God.** Moreover, He is fiercely committed to your growth, healing, calling, and eternity.

Keep walking, even if you are limping, if it is crawling, or if you feel like you have lost more than you have gained.

Keep walking because Jesus, who met Peter on the water, is walking with you now. The same Spirit who raised Christ from the dead is alive in you. Moreover, the same Father who calmed storms then is anchoring you now.

Storms will come. But so will **victory**.

Let me know if you want to trim, split this chapter into two parts, or start the next one!

Chapter 6: Testimonies of Faith and Miracles

From the time of Christ throughout history, many have heard voices and seen miracles in the form of angelic visitations, miraculous healings, and divine blessings through unwavering faith. These accounts, drawn from the pages of Scripture and contemporary lives, reaffirm one vital truth: God still performs wonders. These are not simply inspirational tales but proof that faith is powerful. These testimonies serve as spiritual signposts for those struggling with doubt, fear, illness, or hardship, reminding us that faith truly does move mountains.

Historical Testimonies of Unshakable Faith

Faith is not merely a passive belief but a resilient trust in the unseen. Corrie ten Boom, a Dutch Christian who, along with her family, helped Jews escape the Holocaust during World War II, stands as one of the 20th century's most outstanding examples of living faith. Arrested by the Nazis and sent to Ravensbrück concentration camp, Corrie was subjected to horrific cruelty and suffering. However, through all the despair, she clung tightly to the promises of God. Her quote, "There is no pit so deep that God's love is not deeper still," resonates as a testimony of divine presence amid hellish circumstances.

Corrie's release from the concentration camp came not by her doing, but through what appeared to be a clerical error—an error that spared her from imminent execution. Shortly after, all the women in her age group were executed. This miraculous escape, later confirmed by camp officials, underlines the belief that divine intervention is not just a relic of biblical times.

Biblical Miracles That Inspire Belief

The Bible is rich with testimonies of faith being rewarded with miraculous outcomes. One of the most profound examples is that of the widow of Zarephath in 1 Kings 17. With starvation looming and just a handful of flour and oil left, she planned to prepare one final meal for herself and her son. However, the prophet Elijah then appeared and asked her to use her last resources to bake him bread. It was a request that defied logic, but the widow obeyed in faith. God rewarded her trust by ensuring that her flour and oil never ran out until the drought ended.

This story powerfully reminds us that God's provision is unlocked by obedience in faith. The widow's story is not simply about physical sustenance but a lesson in spiritual abundance. In times of lack, the faithful often experience the richest provision materially, spiritually, and emotionally.

Angels Among Us: Supernatural Encounters

Many believers have historically reported encounters with angels—divine messengers sent to protect, deliver, or communicate God's will. One modern-day example includes a man who, after a severe car accident in a remote location, was pulled to safety by a stranger who disappeared without a trace. Emergency responders later confirmed that no one else had been at the scene. Such stories defy natural explanation but align perfectly with biblical descriptions of angelic intervention.

The Bible is filled with angelic visitations: Gabriel appearing to Mary, angels comforting Jesus in Gethsemane, and the angel who released Peter from prison. These divine encounters serve as reminders that God's care is intimate and personal. Faith does not always result in visible angelic help, but trusting God opens the door to His intervention in ways we may not always understand.

Modern Miracles: Contemporary Accounts of God's Hand

Faith is not just a concept of the past but a living, breathing force in the present. Numerous individuals today testify to miracles that cannot be explained by science or coincidence. Some speak of terminal illnesses healed after prayer, unexplained peace during life-threatening crises, or divine protection during accidents.

Consider a woman diagnosed with stage-four cancer who refused to give up. Her community gathered in persistent prayer. Weeks later, during a follow-up scan, doctors found no trace of the tumour. Alternatively, the man who lost his job was drowning in debt and had no food left, only to receive an anonymous envelope with cash to cover rent and groceries for the month. These are not isolated incidents; they are repeated in the lives of countless believers across the globe.

Financial Miracles: Provision in the Eleventh Hour

The Bible says, "My God shall supply all your needs according to His riches in glory by Christ Jesus" (Philippians 4:19). Many have experienced this firsthand. Financial miracles often happen when believers find themselves at a breaking point. These are moments when rent is due, food is scarce, or bills are overwhelming—and a solution appears at the last moment.

One testimony tells of a family that had no money for Christmas. On Christmas Eve, they found groceries and wrapped presents on their doorstep, left by someone they never identified. Another recounts how a struggling single mother received a call offering her a job after months of searching and near eviction. Faith does not always work on our timeline, but God's timing is perfect.

Physical Healings: Restoring the Body Through Prayer

From the New Testament to today, healing has always been one of the most tangible ways God reveals His power. Jesus healed the blind, raised the dead, and made the boring walk. Today, many continue to witness healing through faith and prayer.

There are documented cases of people healed from chronic diseases, paralysis, and even conditions deemed incurable. What makes these stories more than folklore is the alignment of prayer, belief, and results that medical professionals cannot explain. While not all who pray are healed instantly or physically, the miracle often includes emotional peace, strength to endure, or relational reconciliation—all profound testimonies.

Protection in Peril: Stories of Divine Shielding

Another way miracles manifest is in divine protection. Stories abound of believers narrowly escaping disaster—a car crash avoided by seconds, a fall halted by an unseen force, or being spared from violence in places of conflict. One soldier shared that while on duty in a war zone, a bullet passed through his helmet without touching his head. Another woman testified to being prompted by an inner voice to delay leaving her house, only to find out later there was a fatal pile-up on her usual route.

Such protection often comes without fanfare, but its impact is life-changing. Trusting God does not guarantee we will never face danger, but it does mean He is with us. Psalm 91 declares, "He shall give His angels charge over you, to keep you in all your ways."

Peace in Chaos: The Inner Miracle

Perhaps the most overlooked miracle is peace. When everything externally is falling apart—health, finances, relationships—yet the soul remains anchored, that is a miracle. Jesus said in John 14:27, "Peace I leave with you; my peace I give you." This peace is not from the world; it transcends understanding.

One woman, grieving the loss of her child, described how she felt a calm during worship that she could not explain. Another, after losing everything in a house fire, stood amid the ashes and declared, "God is still good." These testimonies are not born of delusion but a deep, unshakeable faith that God is sovereign, even in suffering.

Faith in the Furnace: Triumph in Trial

Faith is not the absence of difficulty but the presence of belief amid difficulty. The story of Shadrach, Meshach, and Abednego in the Book of Daniel tells of men thrown into a fiery furnace for refusing to bow to an idol. They were unharmed, and a fourth figure—believed to be an angel or a pre-incarnate Christ—was seen walking with them.

This story is not just about divine rescue. It is about the presence of God amid suffering. Today, believers endure persecution, poverty, and even martyrdom in some parts of the world. Their faith, tested in fire, becomes a beacon of light. Their stories, often untold, echo the same refrain: God is with us.

Surrender and Breakthrough: Letting Go to Receive

Miracles often follow surrender. Abraham had to be willing to sacrifice Isaac before God provided the ram. Surrendering control, dreams, or timelines is rarely easy but usually necessary. One young man shared that after years of trying to force his career path, he finally surrendered his plans to God. Months later, he found a job that fit his skills and calling.

Surrender is not defeat—it is trusting God to write the story better than we can. That trust sets the stage for a breakthrough.

Reflecting on Your Testimony

This chapter invites you to pause and reflect. What moments in your life have felt like divine interventions? What peace have you known that defied the storm around you? What provisions showed up just in time?

Keeping a journal of your faith journey can open your eyes to miracles you may have overlooked. Sometimes, they come dramatically. Other times, they are found in subtle changes of heart, unexpected friendships, or simply waking up with hope.

Faith magnifies the ordinary into the extraordinary. Moreover, big and small miracles are never too far from those who believe.

Faith That Ripples: How One Testimony Inspires Another

One of the most potent aspects of testimonies is their ability to multiply faith. Others are encouraged to believe when someone shares how God came through for them. A single story of provision, healing, or peace can ignite hope in someone else's darkness.

Churches and Christian communities often share testimonies during services, not to elevate individuals but to glorify God and stir up expectation. Romans 10:17 says, "Faith comes by hearing, and hearing by the word of God." This applies not only to Scripture but also to the living word of God's action in the lives of His people.

Do not hide your testimony. Please share it. Someone, somewhere, is waiting to hear what God has done in your life so that they can trust Him in theirs.

When Miracles Seem Delayed: Trusting in God's Timing

While many testimonies speak of immediate breakthroughs, some involve waiting, sometimes for years. This waiting is not a sign of God's absence, but often part of His divine plan. Joseph in the Old Testament waited years in slavery and prison before becoming second-in-command in Egypt. Hannah prayed for a child for years before giving birth to Samuel.

Delayed answers test the depth of our faith. However, they often also produce the deepest growth. Faith is not about getting what we want when we want it—it is about trusting that God is good, even when we do not yet see the result.

Waiting seasons are not wasted seasons. They are opportunities to deepen prayer, strengthen community, and mature spiritually. In time, even the silence becomes part of the testimony.

Faith That Transcends Death: Miracles at Life's End

Some of the most sacred miracles occur not in healing but in dying. While the world sees death as the final defeat, faith views it as the gateway to eternal life. Those near death and their families often report miraculous peace, visions of heaven, and unexpected reconciliations.

A hospice nurse once shared how a patient who had been bitter and angry most of his life asked for a Bible days before his passing. He spent his final hours in tears—not of fear, but of gratitude—having finally found the Saviour he had long resisted. His daughter, estranged for years, arrived just in time to hear his whispered apology and say she forgave him. He passed away minutes later, holding her hand. That was a miracle—a soul healed more deeply than the body ever could be.

These end-of-life miracles teach us that God's grace extends to the final breath. No one is ever too far gone. The presence of God, even in death, is the ultimate testimony of hope.

Restored Relationships: When God Rebuilds What Was Broken

Faith restores health or finances and can rebuild hearts and homes. Many testimonies revolve around estranged families reunited, broken marriages restored, or friendships healed after years of bitterness.

One powerful example is a man who had not spoken to his father in over two decades. After attending a church service where the message was about forgiveness, he wrote a letter. To his surprise, his father responded. Over time, they rebuilt their bond. Later, the man discovered his father had been praying for that moment for years.

God is in the business of reconciliation. When we forgive, we mirror His love. Moreover, miracles unfold when we allow Him to enter our relationships—sometimes slowly, but always purposefully.

Miracles amid Persecution

In parts of the world today, Christians face brutal persecution. However, some of the most extraordinary testimonies are born in these places of great suffering. Underground churches thrive. Prisoners experience visions. Enemies become brothers in Christ.

A former radical leader in a war-torn region testified that Jesus appeared to him in a dream, telling him to stop shedding innocent blood. He awoke trembling, renounced violence, and sought out a local pastor. Today, he is a missionary in the same region he once terrorised. That transformation was not just a personal miracle—it became a beacon of hope in a dark place.

Faith under fire produces the purest gold. In persecution, God often reveals Himself in supernatural ways, reminding the world that nothing can quench the light of Christ.

Legacy of Faith: Miracles Passed Through Generations

Faith can shape not just one life, but entire generations. Stories passed down from parents to children build an inheritance far greater than material wealth—a legacy of belief. Grandmothers who prayed daily over their families, fathers who stayed faithful through unemployment, and siblings who encouraged one another through dark valleys all contribute to a living testimony that continues to echo.

One powerful example is a missionary family whose ancestors were saved during a revival generations ago. The fire of that moment never burned out—it sparked a chain reaction of faith, obedience, and commitment that has since led to churches being planted, lives transformed, and nations reached. The miracle was not a single event—the enduring faith kept reproducing fruit.

Your story of faith today could be why your grandchildren walk in boldness tomorrow. Testimonies do not fade; they ripple outward, reshaping lives in ways only eternity can fully measure.

The Power of Collective Faith: Miracles in Community

Though personal faith is powerful, something extraordinary happens when believers unite. Scripture reminds us that where two or more gather in His name, God is in the midst (Matthew

18:20). Collective prayer, worship, and belief create an atmosphere ripe for miracles.

One church in a drought-stricken village prayed together for rain, gathering every night despite dry skies. On the tenth night, with clear skies above, a young girl arrived with an umbrella. When asked why, she responded, "We are praying for rain, aren't we?" That night, it poured.

In another town, a community fasted and prayed for a sick child whose prognosis was grim. Against all odds, the child recovered. The miracle was healing and the revival of faith in an entire neighbourhood.

Faith shared is faith multiplied. When communities believe together, they usher in breakthroughs that no individual could bring alone.

Everyday Wonders: Seeing the Divine in the Mundane

Not every miracle is headline-worthy. Sometimes, it is the right friend showing up at the right time. The exact words you needed to hear spoken by a stranger. A song that brings peace in a chaotic morning. A closed door that leads to the right opportunity. These everyday occurrences are often where God hides His fingerprints.

Seeing these moments as miracles requires a shift in perspective. It is choosing to see grace instead of coincidence, providence instead of luck. Faith sharpens our spiritual sight, allowing us to notice God's hand in the ordinary.

The ability to smile through tears, love after betrayal, and trust after trauma are quite miracles. They do not always draw crowds, but they change hearts, restore hope, and testify just as powerfully.

From Pain to Purpose: When Miracles Are Born

Many of the world's most impactful ministries were born from pain. The parent who has lost a child becomes an advocate for others in grief. The woman healed of addiction begins a recovery centre. The man saved from suicide becomes a counsellor for the depressed.

God often uses brokenness as the soil for blessing. What feels like the end is usually the beginning of a testimony that will help countless others. As 2 Corinthians 1:4 says, "[He] comforts us in all our troubles so that we can comfort those in any trouble with the comfort we receive from God."

If you have endured suffering and found God there, do not hesitate to step forward. Your healing may be the answer to someone else's prayer.

Closing Reflection: Living a Testimony of Faith

Miracles, signs, and wonders are not reserved for saints or super-believers. They are available to all who trust God, even imperfectly. Faith is not about having all the answers but believing in the One who does.

This chapter has shown that God's hand moves through history, Scripture, communities, and individuals. Whether in dramatic interventions or gentle nudges, He remains faithful. Let these stories stir your heart to look for Him in your journey. Keep your eyes open, your heart soft, and your faith engaged.

You do not have to perform a miracle to live a miracle. Every act of obedience, every surrendered fear, every hopeful prayer becomes part of your testimony. Moreover, no matter how simple, every testimony reflects the glory of a living God who delights in working wonders through those who believe.

Faith That Grows in Every Season

Faith is not static. It breathes, stretches, wrestles, and matures with every season of life. In seasons of joy, it praises effortlessly; in seasons of sorrow, it clings desperately; and in seasons of waiting, it deepens quietly. Each testimony shared, every miracle witnessed, and every prayer answered strengthens faith's roots, preparing it to weather the storms ahead.

We are called not just to have faith, but to grow it—to nurture it through daily trust, continual prayer, and relentless hope. Just as a tree planted by streams of water yields fruit in season (Psalm 1:3), so does a life rooted in God's faithfulness bear the fruit of enduring testimony.

Passing the Baton: Empowering the Next Generation

Your testimony is not meant to end with you. Each story of divine provision, healing, and restoration is a seed for the next generation. By sharing how God moved in your life, you inspire others to believe in His goodness.

Scripture exhorts us to "tell the next generation" of God's mighty acts. Grandparents, parents, mentors, and friends are responsible for passing down doctrine and living experiences of faith. These stories become spiritual inheritance—building blocks of courage and trust for those who come after us.

Never underestimate the power of sharing your testimony with a child, a friend, or a stranger. One story can ignite a thousand acts of faith.

Faith Until the Finish Line

The Christian journey is a marathon, not a sprint. While some miracles are seen early and some prayers answered quickly, others are fulfilled only at the end of a long, persevering journey.

Paul, writing near the end of his life, declared with confidence, "I have fought the good fight, I have finished the race, I have kept the faith" (2 Timothy 4:7). This enduring faith, tested by trials and refined by fire, becomes the ultimate testimony—a life lived entirely trusting in God's character and promises.

Finishing healthy means holding onto faith through every season: abundance and lack, health and sickness, joy and grief. It means believing in God's goodness, even when the path winds through valleys and dark places.

The Invitation: Step into the Story

Every believer is invited to live a life that testifies to God's ongoing work. You do not have to wait for extraordinary circumstances to declare His goodness. You do not need a platform or an audience. Testimonies are built in kitchens, hospital rooms, classrooms, workplaces, and quiet corners of prayer.

Wherever you are, God is writing His story through you. The question is not whether He is working but whether we are willing to see, trust, and share.

Today, decide to live expectantly. Believe in miracles, both great and small. Be bold in faith, unshakable in trust, and generous with your testimony. In doing so, you become a living letter from God—an open testimony of His faithfulness, love, and power.

Miracles as Daily Dialogue with God

Miracles are not always loud events—they are often intimate whispers. When you pray and suddenly feel peace wash over you, that is a miracle. When a verse you needed most appears in your devotion, God's voice intervenes in daily life. Testimonies do not need spectacle; they need honesty.

Building a lifestyle that invites miracles means cultivating regular conversation with God. Reading Scripture, praying sincerely, and listening with expectation create spiritual sensitivity. Over time, you will see patterns, connections, and divine fingerprints on what once seemed mundane.

God wants to walk with you daily. The more we listen and notice, the more we realise that the miraculous is not the exception—it is the rhythm of a relationship with a faithful God.

The Testimony of Transformation

Perhaps the most significant miracle is not what God does around us, but what He does within us. Changed hearts, renewed minds, healed emotions—these internal transformations are often overlooked, but they are among our most powerful testimonies.

The angry become gentle. The fearful become bold. The broken become whole. These changes are not accidental; they result from encountering a Saviour who rescues and restores. As Paul wrote in 2 Corinthians 5:17, "If anyone is in Christ, he is a new creation. The old has gone, the new is here!"

Your internal growth is a miracle in motion. Whenever you choose forgiveness, courage, or love where there used to be resentment, fear, or bitterness, you are testifying to the living power of Christ within.

Echoes of Eternity: The Final Testimony

One day, each of us will cross into eternity. The ultimate miracle is not temporary healing or provision but eternal salvation through Jesus Christ. Heaven fulfils every promise and is the destination behind every faith journey.

While our testimonies encourage and inspire others here on earth, they echo into eternity. Scripture speaks of a "cloud of witnesses" (Hebrews 12:1)—those whose lives still speak from beyond the grave. Your faith, your obedience, your trust—these are eternal investments. They matter forever.

When we finally stand before God, we will realise that every act of faith, answered prayer, and whispered worship was heard, recorded, and celebrated in heaven.

Live your testimony now with eternity in mind. Because the story God is writing in you doesn't end here—it's only just begun.

Testimonies as Spiritual Warfare

Every testimony of God's goodness is a weapon against the forces of darkness. Revelation 12:11 proclaims, "They triumphed over him by the blood of the Lamb and by the word of their testimony." When believers declare what God has done, they dismantle fear, doubt, and despair.

Testimonies remind the enemy that he is defeated. They infuse courage into weary hearts. They stir up faith where hope has faded. Speaking about God's faithfulness is not just encouragement but active spiritual warfare. It releases victory into atmospheres of oppression and discouragement.

Never underestimate the power of your story. Your testimony is a sword in the Spirit's hand, cutting through lies and leading others into freedom.

The Ripple Effect of Radical Faith

Faith, when exercised boldly, has a ripple effect far beyond what we can see. A single act of trust can inspire dozens, hundreds, or even thousands. Think of Abraham's obedience—it birthed a nation. Think of Esther's courage—it saved a people.

Modern testimonies reveal the same pattern. One person's decision to believe can alter families, communities, and future generations. Radical faith challenges the status quo, pushes back darkness, and invites heaven to invade earth.

Your radical obedience today could catalyse someone else's miracle tomorrow. Step out boldly, trust fiercely, and let your faith send ripples that transform lives.

Living as a Walking Miracle

Every believer is a walking miracle. Rescued from sin, adopted into God's family, filled with His Spirit—we carry the evidence of divine intervention in our very being.

Living as a walking miracle means approaching each day with gratitude and expectation. It means recognising that your existence is a testimony, your endurance is a declaration, and your transformation is a beacon.

You are living proof that God's power is absolute, His promises are true, and His love is unfailing. Walk boldly in that identity. Let your life be a living letter, read by all, declaring the goodness and faithfulness of your Heavenly Father.

When the Impossible Becomes Reality

Miracles often dwell in the realm of the impossible. They break through the boundaries of human logic, medical certainty, financial limitation, and emotional trauma. When the impossible becomes reality, it serves as a signpost—something supernatural has occurred.

Consider the testimony of a man who was told he would never walk again after a spinal injury. Confined to a wheelchair, he was told his condition was irreversible. But he continued to pray, surrounded himself with a faith-filled community, and refused to give up hope. During a worship service, he felt heat surge through his legs one day. He stood for the first time in years. Doctors were stunned. What science could not explain, faith could.

These moments become milestones. They remind the world that God operates outside human constraints. They remind believers that faith does not ignore reality—it invites a higher reality to intervene. Moreover, for those who witness such transformation, they are never the same again. The impossible, through God, becomes living proof of divine authority.

Such testimonies serve a dual purpose: they glorify God and awaken others to what is possible. When we hear about a marriage restored after betrayal, a terminal illness reversed, or a barren woman giving birth, we are forced to ask, "Could God do that for me, too?" The answer is always yes, if it serves His purpose and strengthens His kingdom.

God is still in the business of doing the impossible. We are called to believe, ask boldly, and testify without shame when He moves. The impossible becomes unforgettable, and miracles dwell in that place.

Faith That Redefines Identity

One of the most profound miracles of faith is the transformation of identity. We are no longer defined by our past failures, sins, or shortcomings when we encounter God. Instead, we are given a new name, a new nature, and a new destiny.

Throughout Scripture, we see God redefine identities. Abram became Abraham—the father of nations. Jacob, the deceiver, became Israel—the one who wrestles with God and prevails. An impulsive fisherman, Simon became Peter, the rock on which Christ would build His Church.

Our testimonies are often born from this radical transformation. God takes the broken pieces of our lives and creates something beautiful. The person with an addiction becomes a counsellor. The orphan becomes a beloved child. The persecutor becomes a preacher.

This change is not merely behavioural; it is foundational. It reshapes how we see ourselves, how we live, and how we interact with the world. No longer bound by shame, fear, or defeat, we walk in the freedom of our true identity in Christ.

One woman shared her testimony of growing up believing she was worthless. Years of emotional abuse left her broken and hopeless. But encountering Jesus changed everything. Through Scripture and the love of the Christian community, she came to see herself as chosen, loved, and valuable. Today, she leads a ministry helping others find their worth in Christ.

This redefinition is ongoing. As we grow in faith, God continues to peel back layers of falsehood and reveal more profound truths about who we are in Him. Each revelation becomes a testimony, a chapter in the greater story of redemption.

Living in our new identity means rejecting the lies that once held us captive. It means embracing the truth that we are fearfully and wonderfully made (Psalm 139:14), that we are more than conquerors through Him who loved us (Romans 8:37), and that we are seated with Christ in heavenly places (Ephesians 2:6).

Faith that redefines identity is a miracle because it changes our lives. It shifts our destiny from despair to hope, from defeat to victory, from wandering to purpose.

As we live out this new identity, our lives become living testimonies. We become walking invitations for others to encounter the same transformative love. Our words and actions declare that no one is too broken, lost, or far gone for God's redemptive power.

Your identity is not found in your past, failures, or wounds. It is found in Christ alone. Let His truth redefine you. Let your life testify to the miracle of a new creation.

Every step you take in your true identity is a declaration of God's miraculous work. Moreover, every testimony of transformation strengthens the body of Christ and expands the kingdom of God.

Miracles Hidden in Small Beginnings

It is easy to celebrate grand, headline-worthy miracles. But some of God's most profound moves begin in places so small, so insignificant to the human eye, that they are almost missed. God delights in using what the world deems insignificant to accomplish the extraordinary.

Consider the mustard seed, one of the smallest of all seeds. Yet Jesus taught that when planted and nurtured, it grows into a tree where birds come and find shelter (Matthew 13:31-32). Likewise, many testimonies start with small, invisible acts: a whispered prayer, a kind word spoken in faith, a decision to forgive, a tiny offering given with great sacrifice.

The miracle often isn't visible at first. It germinates in hidden places. The healing process starts with a single moment of surrender. The restoration of a marriage begins with one heartfelt apology. The financial breakthrough starts with a small act of generosity. Tiny seeds planted in faith often produce harvests beyond imagination.

One woman shared how, after feeling overwhelmed by depression, she made a simple decision each morning: to write down three things she was grateful for. It seemed so insignificant at first. But over time, that daily act transformed her mindset. Joy slowly returned. Hope slowly rekindled. Years later, she now helps others struggling with depression by teaching the power of gratitude.

God specialises in beginnings that seem too small to matter. Moses was a stuttering fugitive when God called him to deliver Israel. David was a forgotten shepherd boy when Samuel anointed him king. Mary was a teenage girl from a humble village chosen to bear the Messiah.

In your own life, do not despise small beginnings. That tiny step of faith you take today might be the seed of a testimony that will inspire generations. That one prayer, one act of obedience, and one seemingly insignificant choice to believe are sacred moments where heaven touches earth.

Nurture your seeds, water them with prayer, shine light on them through Scripture, shield them from doubt and discouragement, and trust that what is unseen today will one day burst forth with visible, undeniable fruit.

Miracles hidden in small beginnings remind us that God sees differently than we do. He looks not at the outward appearance, but at the heart (1 Samuel 16:7). He values faithfulness in little things because they prepare us for greater responsibilities.

If you feel overlooked or insignificant, know this: you are in a prime position for God to do something extraordinary. The quiet acts of obedience you sow today build a harvest you cannot yet see.

Stay faithful in the small. Rejoice over every tiny evidence of growth. Celebrate the unseen hand of God moving beneath the surface. Because in due time, your testimony will bloom—and the world will marvel at what God did through what once seemed so small.

Conclusion: The Power and Purpose of Testimonies

As we close this chapter, let us pause and take in the vast tapestry that has unfolded. Each testimony—whether of miraculous healing, divine provision, supernatural peace, restoration of relationships, or transformation of identity—is more than just a story. It is a revelation of God's character. A testimony is a living declaration that God is not distant or indifferent but deeply involved in the lives of those who seek Him.

Through this journey, we have seen that miracles are not limited to ancient scripture. They are present, ongoing, and accessible to anyone who believes. God is still speaking, healing, delivering, and empowering. The purpose of these acts is not just to bless individuals but to draw others into a greater understanding of His love, mercy, and power.

One remarkable truth we've discovered is that faith is the consistent thread that runs through every testimony. It is the doorway through which the supernatural becomes reality. Whether the widow at Zarephath offering her last meal in faith or the persecuted believer finding strength in a prison cell, faith made space for God to act.

Even more compelling is the realisation that testimonies are not only personal victories—they are communal catalysts. Every testimony has the power to awaken faith in someone else. That's why sharing your story is not a suggestion; it's a commission. Revelation 12:11 reminds us that the people of God overcame the enemy by "the blood of the Lamb and the word of their testimony." Our words carry power. Our stories carry freedom.

We also learned that miracles are not always instantaneous or dramatic. Some happen quietly, over time, in places hidden from the spotlight. Miracles in small beginnings, silent prayers, and gentle restorations are equally valid and robust. The world may overlook these acts, but heaven celebrates every seed of faith that bears fruit.

Throughout the chapter, we encounter people who receive miracles and those who become miracles. This is perhaps the most profound takeaway: we are not just recipients of God's grace—we are vessels of it. A walking testimony embodies hope for the hopeless, light in the darkness, and healing in broken places. It is someone who says, through their life, "God did it for me—He can do it for you."

However, we must also acknowledge that not every story has a perfect earthly ending. Some battles remain unhealed, and some prayers seem unanswered. However, even here, testimonies rise. The testimony is not always in the outcome but in the endurance. It is in the peace that surpasses understanding, the joy that defies circumstances, and the faith that refuses to let go.

As you close this chapter, ask yourself: What is your testimony? What has God done in your life that someone else needs to hear? You may not feel like your story is extraordinary, but remember—ordinary stories in the hands of an incredible God become world-changing testimonies.

Moreover, if you are still waiting for your miracle, take heart. This chapter is not just about looking back—it is about looking forward. Your story is still being written. Miracles often come in unexpected moments, through unanticipated means, and for unforeseen purposes. Stay faithful. Stay hopeful. Keep testifying, even if you are testifying in advance.

Let this chapter ignite something more profound in your spirit—
a hunger to know God more, to believe more boldly, and to
declare His works without hesitation. May you never grow tired
of expecting the miraculous, and may your life become a
wellspring of testimonies that glorify God and inspire others.

Because in the end, testimonies are not just stories—they are
sacred echoes of heaven touching earth, and your voice is
meant to join that chorus.

Chapter 7: Embracing Peace and Purpose

The Divine Pattern in Our Pain

Every soul walks a path carved by joy and sorrow, victories and wounds. However, while the terrain may differ, one truth is common to all: **our struggles are not without meaning**. We serve a God who never wastes pain.

When we face hardship, our minds default to questions: *"Why me?"* or *"What did I do wrong?"* However, Scripture reminds us that suffering is not punishment but preparation. In **Romans 8:28**, we are comforted:
"And we know that in all things God works for the good of those who love him, who have been called according to his purpose."

That "good" may not be ease or comfort—a deeper faith, a stronger character, or a calling we did not anticipate.

In surrendering to God's plan, we begin embracing peace and discovering divine purpose.

The Silent Sculptor: How God Shapes Us

Imagine a block of marble — unremarkable, unformed. In the hands of a sculptor, however, it becomes a masterpiece. But only through chiseling, cutting, and carving.

God is that Sculptor. Moreover, we are His creation.

The trials we face are the tools He uses to shape us. **Isaiah 64:8** says:
"We are the clay, you are the potter; we are all the work of your hand."

This shaping process often feels like breaking, but it is not destruction, but transformation.

God strips away pride, selfishness, fear, and complacency. He exposes our wounds so they can be healed. He dismantles our idols so we can worship Him alone. It is a process of love, even when it hurts.

A Lesson from Joseph: Betrayal to Blessing

Joseph's story is more than a tale of perseverance — it is a roadmap to understanding God's mysterious but perfect purpose in suffering.

- Betrayed by his brothers

- Sold into slavery

- Imprisoned for a crime he did not commit

- Forgotten by those he helped

However, never once did Joseph curse God. He chose faith over bitterness, patience over revenge.

Years later, Joseph would tell his repentant brothers in **Genesis 50:20**:
"You intended to harm me, but God intended it for good to accomplish what is now being done, saving many lives."

Joseph's pain was the very platform for his purpose. Likewise, your deepest pain may be preparing you for your highest calling.

When God Feels Silent

There are seasons in life when God feels distant. Prayers echo unanswered, and circumstances worsen instead of improving. It is tempting to believe that God has turned His face away.

However, silence does not mean absence.

Lamentations 3:25-26 gently reassures us:
"The Lord is good to those whose hope is in him, to the one who seeks him; it is good to wait quietly for the salvation of the Lord."

In these quiet seasons, God teaches us to walk by **faith**, not feelings.

He is still there — in every breath, every tear, every moment you feel alone. His silence invites him to draw nearer, trust deeper, and surrender fully.

Embracing Trials: Not as Punishment but Process

We often see trials as setbacks. However, what if they are set-ups? What if every valley leads us to a higher mountain?

James 1:2-4 exhorts:
"Consider it pure joy, my brothers and sisters, whenever you face trials of many kinds because you know that testing your faith produces perseverance."

Faith is like a muscle. It only grows stronger when stretched.

Every hardship is a classroom. Pain teaches us compassion. Loss teaches us surrender. Unanswered prayers teach us patience. Moreover, broken dreams teach us that God's dreams are better.

God is far more concerned with our character than our comfort. Thus, He allows fire, not to destroy, but to refine.

The Peace That Passes Understanding

Peace in Scripture is not the absence of difficulty; it is the presence of God in the middle of it.

Philippians 4:6-7 teaches us:
"Do not be anxious about anything, but in every situation, by

prayer and petition, with thanksgiving, present your requests to God. Moreover, the peace of God, which transcends all understanding, will guard your hearts and minds in Christ Jesus."

This piece does not make sense — that is its beauty.

It is the peace that steadies you when your world is falling apart. The peace that lets you sleep when storms rage. The peace that reminds you: *God is in control.*

This peace is not earned. It is received. Moreover, it starts with surrender.

The Wilderness Way: Preparation for Purpose

Every person used mightily by God spent time in the wilderness.

- **Moses** spent 40 years in the desert before leading Israel.

- **David** fled from Saul for years before becoming king.

- **Jesus** fasted in the wilderness before beginning His ministry.

The wilderness is not a waste — it is a womb. It births intimacy, dependence, and obedience.

God isolates us to insulate us from distractions. He takes us to quiet places so His voice becomes louder than the world's noise.

So, if you are in a wilderness now, rejoice. You are in divine company.

From Faith to Fruitfulness

Faith is not just belief. It is a movement. It is obedience.

Hebrews 11 recounts people who *did* things because they believed:

- **Abraham** left his home.

- **Noah** built the ark.

- **Rahab** sheltered the spies.

Their faith was not private. It produced fruit.

We must ask ourselves: Is my faith passive or active? Does it show how I love, serve, give, and forgive?

Faith is not just a whisper in the dark — it is a declaration of trust that drives every decision.

Surrendering the Illusion of Control

One of the most brutal truths to accept is this: **we are not in control**.

We plan, we strive, and we hold tightly to our goals. However, peace comes when we loosen our grip.

Jesus demonstrated this surrender in **Luke 22:42**:
"Not my will, but yours be done."

To embrace peace and purpose, we must surrender our plans. It may feel like a loss, but it is a gain — because God's way is always better.

Living With Eternity in Mind

Much of our anxiety stems from short-sightedness. We focus on earthly problems and forget we were made for eternity.

2 Corinthians 4:17-18 offers perspective:
"For our light and momentary troubles are achieving an eternal glory that far outweighs them all... So we fix our eyes not on what is seen, but on what is unseen."

When we view trials in light of eternity, they become bearable — even beautiful.

Eternity reminds us that this life is not all there is. There is more. Moreover, it is glorious.

Finding Purpose in the Pain

Purpose is not found in titles or status. It is found in surrender.

God uses the broken, the bruised, and the overlooked. Your pain may be the very platform from which He speaks to others.

As Paul wrote in **2 Corinthians 12:9**:
"My grace is sufficient for you, for my power is made perfect in weakness."

When we stop hiding our scars, God uses them to heal others.

Let your story — even the messy parts — become a message of hope.

God's Promises Still Stand

Life changes. People leave. Circumstances shift. However, one thing remains: **God's promises never fail.**

Joshua 21:45 assures us:
"Not one of all the Lord's good promises to Israel failed; every one was fulfilled."

What God has spoken over your life will come to pass — in His time, in His way.

Your job is not to figure it all out, but to remain faithful, expectant, and surrendered.

The Power of Perspective

How we view our pain changes how we experience it.

Instead of asking, *"Why is this happening to me?"* ask: *"What is God doing through this?"*

Instead of seeing a delay as denial, see it as preparation. Instead of seeing silence as rejection, see it as refinement.

Perspective does not change the situation, but it changes us.

Practical Ways to Embrace Peace Daily

1. **Begin with Gratitude** – Thank God for three things each day. Gratitude shifts focus from pain to promise.

2. **Meditate on Scripture** – Let God's Word renew your mind. Verses like Psalm 23, Isaiah 41:10, and John 16:33 are anchors.

3. **Pray Honestly** – Pour out your heart without filter. God welcomes raw, unpolished prayers.

4. **Worship in the Waiting** – Praise is powerful. It lifts your spirit and reminds you who's in control.

5. **Serve Someone Else** – Helping others in pain brings healing and perspective.

Living with Purpose Through Seasons of Waiting

Waiting seasons can feel like wasted time, but in God's hands, they are sacred ground. Many people in Scripture fulfilled their purpose *after long delays*:

- **Abraham** waited 25 years for Isaac.

- **David** waited over a decade after being anointed before becoming king.

- **Jesus** waited 30 years to begin His ministry.

God isn't in a hurry — He works in seasons. What feels like a delay is often a time of preparation.

Use your waiting seasons to grow faith, deepen prayer, and develop character. **Galatians 6:9** reminds us:

*"Let us not become weary in doing good, for at the proper time
we will reap a harvest if we do not give up."*

The purpose doesn't disappear during the wait. It matures.

Letting Go of the Need to Understand Everything

Faith does not require complete understanding — it requires
full trust.

We often demand explanations from God, but He offers us the
revelation of His heart, not always His logic. He calls us not to
figure everything out but to **follow Him**, even in the dark.

Proverbs 3:5-6 teaches:
*"Trust in the Lord with all your heart and lean not on your
understanding..."*

When we let go of needing answers, we open ourselves to
peace. Understanding brings control, but trust brings intimacy.

God is not a puzzle to be solved — He is a Father to be trusted.

Turning Pain into Intercession

One of the most powerful things a believer can do with their
pain is to **turn it into prayer**, not just for themselves but also for
others.

When you've suffered loss, you know how to pray for the
grieving. When you've battled depression, you can pray from
the depths for those in darkness. When betrayed, you pray for
the brokenhearted with fierce compassion.

Pain makes our prayers tender, honest, and urgent.

Job 42:10 shows a hidden mystery:
*"After Job had prayed for his friends, the Lord restored his
fortunes and gave him twice as much as he had before."*

Healing flows through intercession. Don't waste your pain —
invest it in prayer.

Building a Life that Radiates Peace

Peace isn't just something we feel — it's something we live out.
A peaceful person influences their environment. Their presence
calms storms, mends conflicts, and restores hope.

Jesus said in **Matthew 5:9**,
*"Blessed are the peacemakers, for they shall be called children
of God."*

Here is how to be a peacemaker:

- **Speak slowly** and listen fully.

- **Refuse gossip** and bring truth with gentleness.

- **Apologize quickly** and forgive freely.

- **Bring calm**, not chaos, into conversations.

When we radiate peace, we become walking testimonies of
God's presence.

Embracing Daily Dependence

Modern culture prizes independence, but spiritual maturity
grows through *dependence on God*, daily, hourly, moment by
moment.

Jesus taught us to pray in **Matthew 6:11**,
"Give us this day our daily bread."

He didn't say weekly or monthly — but daily. Why?

Because peace comes not from storing up enough for tomorrow
but trusting Him sufficient for today.

This daily dependence keeps us humble, focused, and connected to our Source. It moves us away from anxiety and into a rhythm of trust.

Faith That Forgives

One of the greatest hindrances to peace is **unforgiveness**.

When we carry offense, we have unrest. Forgiveness isn't saying what happened was okay — it's saying you refuse to let it poison your heart.

Jesus modeled radical forgiveness: *"Father, forgive them, for they know not what they do."* (Luke 23:34)

When we forgive, we free ourselves. We unchain our joy. We unlock our purpose.

Ask God to help you release the offense, no matter how deep. Let Him heal what you cannot fix.

Peace flows through forgiveness.

The Gift of Sacred Stillness

God often speaks in whispers, not shouts. In a noisy world, stillness becomes sacred.

Psalm 46:10 says:
"Be still, and know that I am God."

Stillness is not laziness. It's intentional resting in His presence.

Set aside a few minutes each day to:

- Turn off all screens

- Close your eyes

- Breathe deeply

- Say nothing — *be* with Him

This stillness re-centers your soul. It silences fear and amplifies His voice.

A Legacy of Peace and Purpose

What we choose today determines what legacy we leave tomorrow.

Do we want to be remembered for anxiety, ambition, peace, love, and unwavering faith?

When we live purposefully, trust God's process, and walk in peace, our lives leave a fragrance that outlasts us.

Paul's prayer in **2 Thessalonians 3:16** is a perfect closing desire for all of us:
"Now may the Lord of peace himself give you peace at all times and in every way. The Lord be with all of you."

Let our lives echo this prayer — daily, humbly, joyfully.

Let peace guard your heart. Let purpose fuel your steps. And let your life become a testimony that even broken things, in God's hands, become beautiful.

Walking with Peace Through Grief and Loss

Grief often feels like the enemy of peace. When we lose someone we love, or when something precious slips through our hands — a dream, a relationship, a season — the heart aches in places words cannot reach.

But even in grief, God promises comfort.
Matthew 5:4 says, *"Blessed are those who mourn, for they will be comforted."*

Peace doesn't mean pretending you're okay. It means knowing that even in your tears, God is near. He weeps with you, walks

with you, and, in time, gently turns mourning into dancing
(Psalm 30:11).

You don't "get over" loss — but with God, you grow through it.

Let your grief become a place of encounter. Let your tears be
seeds of empathy, wisdom, and deep compassion for others.

Raising the Next Generation with Faith and Peace

Our choices today create ripples across future generations.
Whether you're a parent, mentor, teacher, or spiritual example,
your peace and purpose influence others more than you realize.

Children watch how we handle setbacks, and young believers
observe how we respond to conflict. The next generation is
looking not for perfection but for authenticity.

Deuteronomy 6:6-7 instructs:
*"These commandments that I give you today are to be on your
hearts. Impress them on your children..."*

Speak life. Model forgiveness. Show resilience in trials. And
most of all — let them see you trust God when it doesn't make
sense.

That legacy will live longer than your words.

Anchoring Your Identity in Christ

Much of our inner unrest comes from misplaced identity. We tie
our worth to what we achieve, what we look like, or what
others think.

But true peace begins when our identity is anchored in Christ
alone.

2 Corinthians 5:17 declares:
*"If anyone is in Christ, the new creation has come: The old has
gone, the new is here!"*

You are not your past, your performance, your failure, or even your success.

You are:

- Redeemed
- Chosen
- Loved
- Called
- Enough

The world tells you to *"find yourself."* Jesus tells you to *"lose yourself in Me and discover who you truly are."*

Choosing Joy Daily

Peace and joy walk hand in hand. Joy is not giddiness or shallow happiness. It is a deep, unwavering gladness rooted in Christ's presence.

Joy is a choice — a spiritual discipline.

Nehemiah 8:10 proclaims:
"The joy of the Lord is your strength."

Joy sustains us in suffering. It silences fear. It glorifies God.

You can choose joy even when:

- You are uncertain
- You are tired
- You are grieving
- You are waiting

Joy does not deny the pain — it rises amid it.

Wake up each morning and declare, *"Today I choose joy."* It will shift your atmosphere and strengthen your soul.

Recognizing the Voice of Peace

God's voice is not chaotic or accusatory — it brings peace.

1 Kings 19:12 reminds us that God's voice came to Elijah in a gentle whisper, not in fire or storm.

Learn to discern:

- The enemy accuses; God convicts and restores.

- The world rushes; God invites you to rest.

- Anxiety says, "What if?"; Peace says, "Even if."

Spend time in Scripture, worship, and silence. Over time, you will recognize His whisper more easily, especially when you need guidance.

Peace is one of the clearest indicators that you are walking in step with God.

Courage as a Companion to Peace

Peace is not passive — it is powerful. It empowers us to act with courage.

Joshua 1:9 says,
"Be strong and courageous. Do not be afraid... for the Lord your God will be with you wherever you go."

Courage is not the absence of fear — it's choosing obedience despite it. And when we are grounded in God's peace, courage flows naturally.

Courage means:

- Speaking the truth in love

- Saying yes to a calling that scares you

- Forgiving someone who doesn't deserve it

- Walking into the unknown, trusting God holds it

Courage and peace are not opposites — they are siblings, born from trust in God.

Rest as a Sacred Rhythm

In a culture that glorifies hustle, rest is revolutionary.

God modeled rest after creation, and Jesus withdrew often. Rest is not laziness—it's alignment with God's design.

Exodus 33:14 says:
"My Presence will go with you and give you rest."

Rest:

- Resets your mind

- Renews your body

- Refreshes your spirit

- Reminds you that you are not God — He is

Make space for sacred rest — not just physically, but spiritually. Lay down burdens. Cease striving. Let His peace flood your soul.

Enduring to the End with Unshakable Purpose

Many begin the journey of faith with fire but struggle to finish well. Life's weariness can dull passion. But those who endure with peace and purpose leave the most impact.

Hebrews 12:1-2 calls us to:
"Run with perseverance the race marked out for us, fixing our eyes on Jesus, the pioneer and perfecter of faith."

You will face setbacks. You may fall. But get up. Refocus. Keep running.

You were not called to survive — you were called to overcome.

And one day, you'll hear the words that make every tear and every trial worth it:
"Well done, good and faithful servant." (Matthew 25:23)

The Fireproof Soul: Thriving in Adversity

Adversity tests faith and tempers it, like gold in the furnace. Just as fire refines metal, so trials refine our trust in God. A fireproof soul does not avoid the flames, but one that walks through them without being consumed.

Isaiah 43:2 says: "When you walk through the fire, you will not be burned; the flames will not set you ablaze."

A fireproof soul:

- Praises through the pain

- Chooses faith over fear

- Worships when nothing makes sense

- Believes that God is good even in the dark

Shadrach, Meshach, and Abednego were thrown into the fire — but they were not alone. Jesus was with them in the furnace. Your fiery season may feel lonely, but you are never abandoned. The fire you fear may be where God walks closest to you.

When Faith Feels Fragile

There are moments when faith doesn't feel like a mighty roar, but a whisper. It trembles. It questions. It doubts.

But fragile faith is still faith.

Jesus said in Matthew 17:20: "If you have faith as small as a mustard seed... nothing will be impossible for you."

Your strength is not in how *big* your faith is, but in **who** your faith is in.

God honors even the smallest step forward. He sees the tearful prayer, the shaky yes, and the quiet surrender, and He meets them with grace.

Don't be ashamed of fragile faith. It's real. It's honest. And it's often the beginning of a breakthrough.

Carriers of Peace in a Chaotic World

Those who walk in peace are rare and radiant in a world of division, anxiety, and noise.

Philippians 2:15 challenges us to "shine like stars in the sky" in a warped generation.

You don't have to preach loudly or post boldly to make a difference. Sometimes peace itself is your loudest witness.

When others panic, you trust.

When others argue, you listen.

When others seek revenge, you forgive.

This kind of peace is not weakness — it's warfare. It fights against fear, hate, and despair with the steady presence of God within.

Be a carrier of peace. Let people feel calmer, safer, and more loved after encountering you. That's ministry.

The Strength of Still-Standing

Sometimes, victory doesn't look like conquering mountains — it looks like standing when everything in you wants to fall.

Ephesians 6:13 urges, "...having done everything, to stand."

Standing doesn't mean you feel strong. It doesn't mean you understand what God is doing. It means you still hold on to hope, faith, and truth.

When you've prayed and nothing has changed
When you've hoped and still hurt
When you've tried again and again but haven't seen a breakthrough

— Just standing is sacred.

The enemy wants you to quit. God asks you to stay. Because every time you choose not to give up, you declare: "My God is still worthy — even in the waiting."

Sacred Scars: Your Story is Your Strength

We often try to hide our scars — physical, emotional, and spiritual. But in God's kingdom, scars are testimonies. They say, "I've been wounded... but also healed."

John 20:27 describes how Jesus still had scars even in His resurrected body. He didn't erase them—He showed them.

Your scars:

- Show survival

- Prove healing is possible

- Speak louder than sermons

Someone needs to know they're not alone; your story may be their survival guide.

Let your scars be sacred. Let them shine with purpose, not shame. What once brought you pain may now bring others peace.

The Promise Beyond the Pain

God doesn't promise a life without pain, but He does promise His presence, purpose, and peace through it all.

Revelation 21:4 shows us the end: "He will wipe every tear from their eyes. There will be no more death or mourning or crying or pain..."

This is not a fantasy. It's a future reality. And it reminds us that our current suffering has an expiration date.

Every ache will be answered. Every tear accounted for. Every faithful step is rewarded.

Keep going — not because it's easy, but because eternity is worth it.

Walking in God's Timing: Trusting the Divine Clock

Waiting for God's timing can seem impossible in a world that thrives on instant gratification. We are accustomed to planning, setting goals, and expecting immediate results. Yet, throughout Scripture, we see that God's timeline rarely aligns with our own. His timing is not slow; it is perfect.

Ecclesiastes 3:1-8 reminds us:
"There is a time for everything, and a season for every activity under the heavens..."

We each have moments when we want to rush ahead, to force our desires into action. We may see others advancing, but God calls us to wait. Trusting His timing does not mean inactivity—it means faithful preparation. Like a farmer waiting for the crops to grow, we are asked to patiently trust that our planted seeds will bloom at the right time.

When we wait on God, we learn to let go of control. We trust that His plan, even though it may seem delayed or mysterious, is working for our good. God's timing does not just affect us—it ripples outward, impacting our family, community, and world. In this waiting, He refines us, builds our endurance, and molds us into people ready to fulfill His purpose.

It is easy to feel impatient when we cannot see what lies ahead. However, God's delay is not a denial. In the story of Abraham, God promised him descendants as numerous as the stars in the sky, but Abraham had to wait for years before he saw the fulfillment of that promise. Moreover, even then, the journey continued. God's timing stretches us beyond our limits and forces us to trust Him in impossible ways when we rush ahead.

The beauty of God's timing is that it is tailored perfectly to the path He has set for us. He knows when we are genuinely ready and the world is prepared for us. Trusting His divine clock requires us to rest assured that the Creator of the universe is not late—He is never early either. He is always right on time.

The Strength Found in Surrender

The concept of surrender often seems counterintuitive, especially in a world that values strength and self-sufficiency. We are taught to push forward, assert our will, and rely on our capabilities. However, true strength is found not in control but in surrendering to God's will regarding peace and purpose.

In Matthew 11:28-30, Jesus offers an invitation:
"Come to me, all weary and burdened, and I will give you rest. Take my yoke upon you and learn from me, for I am gentle and humble, and you will find rest for your souls. For my yoke is easy and my burden is light."

Jesus models this surrender, even in the most challenging moments of His life. In the Garden of Gethsemane, on the night He was to be betrayed, He prayed, "Not my will, but yours be done" (Luke 22:42). This was not a resignation, but a conscious choice to trust the Father with His fate. Jesus understood that true peace comes from yielding to God's plan, even when it involves suffering.

In our lives, surrender does not mean giving up. It does not mean passively accepting everything that comes our way without action. Instead, it means releasing our desires, fears, and ambitions to God. It means accepting that His ways are higher than ours and His purposes are more significant.

Surrendering our plans, goals, and desire for control allows God to do something greater through us and us. It opens the door for His peace to fill our hearts and His power to be perfect in our weakness. The apostle Paul describes this paradox in 2 Corinthians 12:9-10:
"But he said, 'My grace is sufficient for you, for my power is made perfect in weakness.' Therefore, I will boast all the more gladly of my weaknesses, so that the power of Christ may rest upon me. For Christ's sake, I am content with weaknesses, insults, hardships, persecutions, and calamities. For when I am weak, then I am strong."

In surrender, we find a strength that is not our own. We can do things we never thought possible, not by our abilities, but through the power of the Holy Spirit working in us. This strength is rooted in peace—the peace that comes when we stop fighting against God's will and trust Him to lead us where we need to go.

When we surrender, we no longer carry the heavy burden of trying to control everything. Instead, we exchange our burdens for the light yoke of Jesus. The rest He promises is not a cessation of work or struggle, but a deep, abiding peace that sustains us through whatever comes our way. In surrender, we are free to walk in the purpose God has designed for us, without the weight of striving to create our path.

The Power of Prayer in Uncertainty

Amid pain, confusion, or uncertainty, prayer becomes a vital lifeline connecting us to God's heart. When everything around us seems unstable, prayer grounds us in the truth that we are not alone. It is a channel through which God invites us to bring our fears, frustrations, hopes, and desires before Him.

James 5:16 teaches:
"The prayer of a righteous person is powerful and effective."

Prayer does not just change things—it changes us. It shifts our perspective, aligns our hearts with God's will, and invites peace into our lives. In the darkest moments, when we feel overwhelmed by life's uncertainties, prayer is an act of surrender. We declare that we trust God's sovereignty, even when we do not have all the answers.

Jesus exemplified the power of prayer throughout His ministry, especially during intense distress. Before His arrest, in the Garden of Gethsemane, He prayed with such intensity that His sweat became like drops of blood (Luke 22:44). His prayer was a conversation of surrender, trusting the Father to carry out His will, no matter the cost.

For us, prayer offers a similar invitation. It is not a way to manipulate God's will but to align our hearts with His. It is through prayer that we can release our anxieties, and by doing so, experience the peace that surpasses all understanding (Philippians 4:6-7).

In the throes of uncertainty, prayer may not always change our circumstances immediately, but it changes our hearts and ability to trust God's perfect plan. It reminds us that He is not distant but present, walking alongside us through every trial. Prayer draws us closer to His peace, helping us endure with grace and hope.

The Transformative Power of Forgiveness

One of the most powerful and yet most challenging aspects of embracing peace is forgiveness. Forgiveness is releasing someone from the debt they owe us, whether emotional, physical, or spiritual. It is an act of obedience to God's command to forgive, as He has forgiven us.

In Matthew 18:21-22, Peter asked Jesus how often he should forgive a brother who sins against him. Jesus responded, "I tell you, not seven times, but seventy-seven times." This response shows that forgiveness is not a one-time act, but an ongoing choice to release resentment, bitterness, and anger, regardless of the offense.

Forgiveness does not mean that what was done to us is okay or that we must forget. It means choosing to allow no longer the offense to control our hearts and minds. Forgiveness frees us from the bondage of anger and bitterness, and in doing so, it opens the door for peace to reign.

Jesus, in His ultimate act of forgiveness, prayed for His enemies while He was being crucified. In Luke 23:34, He said, "Father, forgive them, for they do not know what they are doing." Jesus showed us that forgiveness depends not on the other person's actions but on obeying God and living in peace.

The transformative power of forgiveness is evident in the life of Corrie ten Boom, a Holocaust survivor who was able to forgive the Nazi soldier who had wronged her family. Through her story, we learn that forgiveness is not only for the benefit of the one being forgiven but primarily for our healing. When we forgive, we are free from the prison of anger and bitterness.

Forgiveness brings peace because it removes the weight of unhealed wounds. It does not come naturally, but with God's help, we can forgive as we have been forgiven. As we forgive, we experience healing, reconciliation, and peace.

Walking in Peace Amidst Conflict

One of the most significant challenges in life is maintaining peace amid conflict. Conflict can easily disturb the peace God offers us, whether in relationships, workplaces, or even within our hearts. However, peace is not the absence of conflict but the ability to remain anchored in God's presence regardless of the turmoil around us.

Romans 12:18 encourages us:
"If possible, as it depends on you, live at peace with everyone."

While we cannot always control others' actions, we can control how we respond. Jesus' example of peace in the face of conflict teaches us to act with humility, gentleness, and love. When falsely accused, He remained silent, trusting the Father to vindicate Him (Matthew 27:12-14). His response was not weakness but strength grounded in His trust in God's justice.

In times of conflict, it is easy to become reactive, to defend ourselves or attack those who hurt us. However, true peace requires us to pause, to seek God's wisdom, and to respond with grace. Proverbs 15:1 reminds us:
"A gentle answer turns away wrath, but a harsh word stirs anger."

Living at peace with others does not mean avoiding difficult conversations or ignoring wrongdoings. It means approaching each situation with a heart that desires reconciliation, understanding, and love. By choosing peace, we reflect God's nature and show the world a different way to handle conflict.

When we respond to conflict with peace, we trust God's sovereignty. We allow Him to fight our battles, knowing He will make things right. Our peace is not dependent on the outcome of the conflict—it is grounded in our trust in God's perfect plan.

Conclusion: Embracing Peace and Purpose

As we come to the end of Chapter 7, it is clear that peace and purpose are inseparable. Our journey toward peace requires us to embrace God's sovereignty in every area of life, surrendering our will to His, and trusting His timing and plan. We find the peace that transcends understanding through surrender, prayer, forgiveness, and a commitment to live in harmony with others.

This peace does not eliminate pain but offers us the strength to endure. It does not remove conflict, but gives us the wisdom and courage to respond gracefully. Most importantly, it enables us to walk in the divine purpose God has prepared for us.

We are reminded that peace is not a passive state but an active pursuit. It requires effort, intentionality, and trust. However, as we seek God's peace, He also grants us His purpose. Our pain, struggles, and trials are not wasted—they are part of shaping us into vessels of His love, truth, and peace.

By embracing peace, we become carriers of that peace to the world around us. Our lives become a reflection of God's goodness, a testimony to His transformative power. Walking with peace and purpose, we fulfill His calling on our lives, impacting His kingdom.

Final Words

There is a sound that escapes the human heart when words are no longer enough. A sound born not in the lips, but in the spirit—a deep, aching cry that rises beyond human ears and enters the courts of heaven. It is the cry of the soul in travail, the groan of one who has reached the end of themselves, and yet—by grace—finds God waiting there.

This cry is not polished. It does not echo in the corridors of the proud. It emerges from the wilderness, from prison cells of circumstance, from the weary and worn who have walked through the fire and the flood. It is the cry of Job, stripped of all comfort, lifting his ash-covered voice: "Though He slay me, yet will I trust Him" (Job 13:15). It is the cry of David, chased and broken, singing from the cave: "I cried unto the Lord with my voice... and He heard me" (Psalm 3:4). It is the cry of Jesus, kneeling in Gethsemane, sweat mingled with blood: "Father, if You are willing, take this cup... nevertheless, not My will, but Yours be done" (Luke 22:42).

This cry-this sacred utterance of surrender-is the very sound that reaches heaven. It is not volume that moves the throne of God, but vulnerability. It is not eloquence, but honesty. It is not strength, but surrender. When we cry out in our weakness, heaven answers in its power. When we are emptied, the fullness of Christ is made known.

We have journeyed through pages of pain, promise, struggle, and sovereignty. The testimonies shared in this book are not neat stories with tidy bows. They are raw, bruised, beautiful testaments to the God who does not leave us in the fire but joins us there—the God who does not merely observe from afar but steps into time, flesh, and suffering—Emmanuel, God with us.

He has been there in the silence of your nights, in the solitude of your questioning, in the exhaustion of waiting. You may not have always seen Him. You may not have felt the answer. However, your cry did not fall to the ground. It rose, like incense, into the very heart of God.

The cry that reaches heaven is not a sign of failure. It is a declaration of faith. It says, "God, I still believe You are good, even when my eyes see nothing but pain." It says, "I will wait, even if the waiting breaks me." It says, "I do not understand, but I trust You anyway."

Moreover, in this cry, heaven responds—not always with immediate answers, but always with presence. "The Lord is near to those who are of a broken heart; and saves those who are crushed in spirit" (Psalm 34:18). His nearness is not conditional on your strength. His love does not wait for you to have it all together. He meets you in the mess. He holds you in the mystery. He walks with you through the valley and sits beside you in the silence.

A sacred truth exists in your suffering: God is not wasting it. Every tear you have cried, He has counted. Every night you have endured, He has seen. Moreover, every cry you have lifted, He has heard.

He is the God who answers by fire, the God who speaks in the storm, the God who heals with a word and restores with a breath. Moreover, even when His answer is not what we expect, it is always what we need. His ways are higher, His thoughts are more profound, and His love is unsearchable.

So now, as this journey comes to its final page, do not close the book thinking your story is over. No, dear soul—your story is still unfolding in the hands of the Author and Finisher of your faith. A Cry That Reached Heaven has set something in motion. Something unseen, but eternal. Something hidden, but holy.

Continue to cry out—not in despair, but in faith. Continue to hope—not in what is seen, but in Him who is unseen. For the God who heard you then still hears you now. Moreover, he is not finished.

Let your cry rise like a song of the broken and beloved.

Let your pain become a prayer.

Let your life become an altar.

Moreover, let this be your confidence: the cry that reaches heaven will never return void.

Amen.